TIME TO REMEMBER
BOOK ONE: ATLANTIS

SANDI PHILLIPS MEYLER

Copyright © 2022 by Sandi Phillips Meyler

All rights reserved.

No part of this book may be reproduced in any form or by any electronic or mechanical means, including information storage and retrieval systems, without written permission from the author, except for the use of brief quotations in a book review.

FREE GIFT

Thank you, friend, for bringing your focus this way! SO much fun to be in it together! Add more tools to your toolkit and continue your expansion as an intentional, masterful creator!

Sign up below and receive a new tool weekly for the next five weeks!

SIGN UP HERE:
https://bit.ly/deliberatecreatorstoolbox

SCAN ME

This book, and this trilogy, is dedicated to our future. I hope to rendezvous with the parallel reality where the USA is the United States of Atlantis, where the utopia of our past, AND our future, is at hand. You, and I, we are all that! See you there!

ACKNOWLEDGMENTS

I gratefully acknowledge all the like-minded others who, like me, pursue mastery of intentional creation and who draw this exciting series through me.

Thank you. It is an honor to acknowledge your light and your power. You are genius, you are brilliant, you are unstoppable.

I'd also like to acknowledge some of the works that form the foundation of my own Deliberate Creation orientation. This includes, but is not limited to, the works of Abraham Hicks, Dr. Joe Dispenza, and Bashar, along with many practitioners of Science of Mind: Ernest Holmes, Michael Beckwith, and John Randolph Price, to name just a few.

CHAPTER 1
ATLANTIS, 10,802 BCE

It was like splashing in puddles of light. Tia stepped happily along the glistening stone street. It was that magic hour of sunrise when the city, still engulfed in mist, was just beginning to wake up. She was on her way to a very special rendezvous, and as she walked she mused, "I love knowing how to use my thoughts and emotions purposefully to create my day!" Tia was well practiced at keeping herself in a state of appreciation, and it was easy for her to find much to deeply appreciate as she walked the streets of her beloved Atlantis, the capital city of the kingdom of the same name. She noticed the paving stones and the way they shimmered in an endless variety of colors, and she appreciated how brilliant the city's planners and designers had been when they decided to dust the tops of those stones with selenium. She appreciated the city's organized system of roads, all leading to a pyramid-shaped building at the precise geometrical city center. That building housed the kingdom's leadership and the seat of power, and as the sun rose behind the pyramid, many people were headed on foot toward their jobs in the central offices. Those she encountered gave Tia the customary quarter bow, acknowledging her as part of the royal order.

Earlier, in her home that doubled as her metalworking shop, Tia had excitedly readied for the much-anticipated day ahead. Looking around at her workspace, her heart swelled with pride in carrying forward her late father's legacy. She spoke lovingly, out loud, to her father's spirit. "I know you are glad that the people of Atlantis who regularly came to you to create items of beauty from precious metals, are now commissioning me with that task and privilege. I love that you can see how I am using the secrets of metal-crafting that you taught me."

Sighing with satisfaction, Tia took a moment to glance at several of the finished pieces in her workshop. They were fashioned from silver, gold, and copper, and some were made from a powerful amalgam called orichalcum. When a mixture of molten silver, gold, and copper was poured into molds to form big sheets of the material, it would harden with a smooth shimmery surface. Most of the buildings in the city of Atlantis and all around the kingdom were made of stone foundations and walls, and many were covered with a layer of orichalcum. The special metal gave the city a lustrous sheen that made it, Tia thought, luxuriously beautiful. And the orichalcum raised the vibration of the citizenry as they moved around and through the buildings.

The items in Tia's workshop ranged from small, delicate pieces of jewelry, to large and imposing projects such as gates and fences. Each was a unique work artistically and energetically, and her heart sang as sweetly when she was designing a toe ring as when she was fashioning a grand entrance arch for the city.

This particular spring morning, however, there would be no metalworking. "My Tenuen and I will be together again today," she thought with shivering anticipation. "My betrothed and I have been separated this time for so many moons," she whispered. Regarding herself in the mirror, she inspected with pleasure the reflection of her tall, sturdy, long-legged frame that possessed a wonderful ease and grace of movement. As a High Priestess of

Atlantis, Tia wore the traditional garments in a deep royal purple. Her dress was lined with handspun silk, and the hem was bordered with embroidered symbols that signified her achievements in her studies of vibrational metaphysics.

Satisfied with her clothing, she looked up at her hair. "I suppose my usual messy braid with a stick shoved through it isn't appropriate today," she mumbled to herself, holding her hair up out of her eyes as she decided what to do. Most days she really couldn't be bothered to wrest it into an orderly hairdo, but today was no ordinary one. Today she would be reunited with her beloved. So she took the time to brush her locks until they smoothly framed her long, broad face in shiny flaxen waves. Her clear blue eyes could capture anyone they gazed at with their intensity, imparting a feeling of nowhere-to-hide. This morning they danced with love and excitement.

As a youngster, besides being an apprentice artisan, Tia had been educated as a child of the priestly order of Atlantis, schooled together with the offspring of the royal family. The children were taught that all beings, objects, and substances on the planet are in constant vibration, each vibrating to its own native resonant frequency. The Atlanteans believed that the most important aspect of physical life experience was orienting one's self toward maintaining alignment with the frequencies that match the beings, objects, and circumstances that were wanted. This was the bedrock for understanding the society Tia lived in. Intentional appreciation for things that were pleasing was what she and her fellow Atlanteans were trained in from birth.

Now, as she made her way along the street, her appreciation of the glistening paving stones and of the way the fabric of her deep purple coat seemed to shift and change colors as she moved, caused the vibration of her being to rise. She fell into a deep reverie as she gave her focused attention to the beauty in the details she observed. She knew that purposefully focusing attention this way would create more pleasing things in her life—more people, things, and circumstances that matched the vibrational frequency of joy.

Tia was truly relaxed and happy as she walked on toward the center of the city. "I even love the name of the kingdom and its capital city," she mused. "Atlantis. It feels cozy and comforting somehow."

CHAPTER 2
TIA AND TENUEN

Tia's focus was drawn away from her surroundings as she turned her thoughts excitedly to her beloved who was at that moment on his way to meet her.

Prince Tenuen of the Kingdom of Atlantis was the youngest of King Aztlan's ten sons. All of the princes bore a striking resemblance to their father and to one another. Their broad, handsome, copper-skinned faces all had strong chins, no facial hair, and penetrating olive-green eyes. In fact, the brothers looked so much alike they were often mistaken one for the other by those who didn't know them well, a fact the mischievous boys capitalized on to no end, even as grown-up royal adults.

When Tenuen thought back to his upbringing in the royal household, which he did often, his memories always featured joy, mirth, and fun. King Aztlan took his responsibilities as leader of the kingdom seriously and responsibly, yet he raised his boys to play. He knew that even when at work, one should play, and that in fact, play was the way they would create success in life. So the Atlantean princes were often known to pull pranks and practical jokes on one another, and they grew up often hearing their elders say, "there is never really anything serious going on."

These teachings did not originate with Tenuen's father. Zeus, paternal grandfather of the ten princes, had been half-mortal and half deity, and as such, he understood the true nature of reality and what physical existence really is all about. His influence kept the royal family steeped in the understanding that all souls are eternal, and that beings come to Earth to experience physical life mostly for the sheer fun of it. A sense of lightheartedness pervaded the royal family home, and Tenuen grew up behaving in accordance with the knowledge that it's always best to "play your way through." "Boys," Grandfather Zeus would say, "it's all just one big cosmic joke we play on ourselves."

This knowing that life was meant to be joyful, humorous, and full of mischief was one of the primary things that endeared him so deeply to Tia. Yet even though Tia understood these things well, it could sometimes bring her to the brink of maddening frustration when she wanted Tenuen to take her seriously about something, and he chose not to.

That didn't matter now. Tenuen often traveled as part of his duties as King Aztlan's ambassador to the other regions of Atlantis. This time he'd been away on a particularly extended trip to the farthest reaches of the kingdom, where he visited the Atlantean regions overseen by his two eldest brothers. Although her life was full and enriching even during Tenuen's frequent absences, Tia was now deeply glad at the thought of his return. She picked up the pace of her walking, raised her gaze from the paving stones, and looked toward her destination—the place she and Tenuen most loved to meet. Tia's heart quickened along with her steps. "Soon! Soon I'll be in his arms!"

The pair was never actually completely separated, of course, since Tia and Tenuen could meet in the quantum non-physical, and often did. All Atlantean citizens had at least a rudimentary understanding of vibrational metaphysics, and Tia and Tenuen, as members of the royal court, were required to continue their studies, in depth, all their lives. They were able to connect energetically and vibrationally even when they were physically far apart. They could reach a specific mental state by way of meditation. Grandfather Zeus had called this state "the field." They didn't have to plan this and synchronize their meditations. Each was able to meet the nonphysical self of the other by entering a meditation with clear intention to do so.

This was where their eternal true natures, what might be called their souls, experienced themselves as pillars of light that danced beyond form and across all time and space. There, in that quantum reality, they were completely untethered and unfettered by physicality, and their energies and light would intertwine in a joyous celebratory dance. Because they had this ability, Tia, accustomed to Tenuen's frequent absences from the city, knew that no matter where their physical bodies were located at any given time, they could always be together in the field. She knew that they had always been, and always would be together this way —before, during and after this particular physical lifetime.

"Today, though," thought Tia, "I get to experience the best of both worlds!"

She loved all the aspects of being in love. And today there would be the added exquisite pleasure of a meeting of their physical selves. "What's this strange sensation in my belly?" She giggled, surprised to find herself almost nervous at the thought of being with Tenuen again. It amazed her that after a lifetime of familiarity, or perhaps because of it, she always had intense physical responses to him.

Tia's heart fluttered again as she approached a tall building that was surrounded by an eight-foot stone wall. This was the largest building in the complex, and served as the main healing facility of Atlantis. Access was gained through gates that were cut into the wall at intervals. The wall was painted on the side facing the city with bright, colorful murals that depicted a glorious and varied garden. The murals were a realistic rendering of the garden that surrounded the healing center just inside the wall, where lush beds of a huge variety of plants and flowers formed an intricate design consisting of all the colors of the rainbow, and giving off a glorious mixture of scents. The outside of the wall was painted in such a way that it vibrated at the same frequency as the actual living garden within—the frequency of well-being and good health. This meant that the vibration of anyone passing by would be positively entrained by the garden's vibration and reap its benefits just as if they had taken a walk through its flowers, trees, and bushes.

In addition to the stone footpaths like the one Tia plied this day, there were openings in the wall that allowed streams of water to flow into the grounds of the building complex and into the buildings themselves. The water was brought from the sea by a series of canals, and like the garden, it provided vital energy and the vibration of thriving to the healing center.

Tia stepped through one of the gates and there she paused at the entrance to the garden, closed her eyes, and breathed deeply to take in the euphoric aroma in the air. Opening her eyes, she started toward her favorite secluded corner of the garden, and looked around to see if her cherished wooden bench was available. Yes, there it was, situated next to the trunk of a beautiful ancient balsam tree. Colorful birds of all sizes would often congregate in that area of the garden, and she always enjoyed watching them, hearing them sing, and feeling the movement of air that their fluttering wings created.

Tia settled herself on the bench feeling bubbly and excited. She felt herself blush from the content of her own thoughts about what was to come. After all, it had been quite a while since she and her betrothed had been physically in one another's arms!

She waited just a few minutes, and there was Tenuen. Looking up at the exact moment that he entered the garden, she saw him walking toward her from the gate. "He is so beautiful!" Tia's breath caught in her chest as she took in the sight of him. "He seems to grow more strikingly handsome as time passes." She drank him in with her eyes as she watched him approach, and when his eyes met hers his face softened and lit up at the same time. Seeing this, Tia could not hold to any pretense of refined behavior. She sprang up and ran the short distance straight into his arms. When he hugged her close to his chest and spun her around, her breath was taken away yet again.

Overflowing with joyful emotion, but not yet speaking, they stumbled together to the bench near the balsam tree. Sitting down, they maintained their eye contact, and clasped hands tightly. They gazed at one another for a long moment, each taking in the other's energy that they'd missed so much. Tenuen's smiling countenance felt like the warmth of the sun on Tia's face.

Usually when they met up in physical after a time of being apart, they would take a romp out into the quantum field before doing anything else, and today was no different. Closing their eyes, together they entered a deep meditative state and glided into the field holding hands. Going into the field with their bodies physically touching made it an even more intense and deep experience than when they met in the field while physically apart. Tia knew that after dancing with abandon with Tenuen in the field, when they returned to their bodies there would be even more sparks than usual flying between them, and they would have a heightened awareness of their physical connection to one another.

When they returned from the field and came back into awareness, their physical bodies were still sitting on the bench, hands clasped. There is no time in the quantum field, so it felt like none had passed.

To Tia, the sensation of being back in her physical body was of complete well-being and exquisite excitement at being alive. Unable to contain herself, she leaped onto Tenuen's lap in one fluid motion that knocked them both, laughing, onto the grass. Joy radiated from them in shimmering colored waves of light that mingled with the shapes and hues of the flowers of the garden.

After a while they settled down and lay side by side on the ground, faces to the sky. Tia turned and beheld her Tenuen, and she noticed that this recent trip seemed to have bestowed certain wisdom on him. She could see and feel a storm of thoughts going on behind his bright green eyes. He noticed her watching him, and responded by wrapping her in a deep bear hug, pulling her as close as he could, so happy to have Tia present and in his arms once more. "There is nothing as thrilling as really being together this way," he thought. Of course, Tenuen knew, just as Tia did, how to use his ability to appreciate and raise his vibration even when Tia was not around. Still... vibrational metaphysics be damned sometimes. He just wanted to hold Tia and bask in the feeling of having her physical body against him.

Tia reveled in the thought that they were breathing the same air and seeing the same sight of the canals gently flowing by, sparkling in the morning sun. Tenuen was almost a full foot taller than Tia, and when they were prone on the grass like this, heads together, her feet reached to just below his knees. Lying with him this way always made her feel protected, safe, and loved.

Tia liked to lay her hand over Tenuen's chest and feel his heartbeat and the life force that flowed through him and from him. As she did that now, she felt and saw the familiar rush of silvery light, and she smiled. But, then she noticed that while the silvery light was still there, this time there was something different, too. Something darker. It was disconcerting and unfamiliar, and did not have the vibrational frequency that she associated with Tenuen. She wanted to dismiss this sensation, but she remembered encountering this feeling earlier that day as well, during their meditation when Tenuen first arrived. She hadn't examined it then, not wanting to turn toward darkness during their dance in the light, but now, as she held her hand to Tenuen's heart, she tried to explore it with curiosity.

CHAPTER 3
INTEGRA

Before any unsettling thoughts and feelings had time to take hold, Tia suddenly felt, as much as she saw the sweeping garments of another high priestess swoosh up to where she and Tenuen were lying near the balsam tree. She knew at once just by the bright crimson hem, embroidered like Tia's own with symbols of achievement in vibrational metaphysics studies, that it was her dear friend, Integra. The Crystal Whisperer, Tia liked to call her.

Integra's slight frame and short stature, along with her black silken hair that covered ears that sometimes looked pointed, left one with the feeling that she was perhaps a pixie, or a fairy. People would often blink and look more closely, only to see that they were mistaken, yet left wondering about it all the same, as if their eyes were playing tricks on them. It always amused Tia when she observed this happening when someone met Integra for the first time, and she giggled to herself every time someone left Integra's presence shaking their head, wondering what they'd just encountered. Integra however, for some reason, didn't seem to notice.

Raised in the same royal circles, Integra and Tia had been in one another's lives from the very beginning. While it was always Tia's intention to love her fellow humans unconditionally, sometimes it took specific focus and intentionality for her to get there. But with Integra, it took no effort at all. Tia cherished the ease, joy and comfort of their friendship and the nonjudgmental acceptance they had for one another.

Tia shaded her eyes with her hand against the morning sun that was now high in the sky, and looked up at her friend. She was happy to see Integra, but at the same time she felt the desire to linger a bit longer in Tenuen's arms and delight in his homecoming. She also wanted to explore her now burning curiosity about that apparent shadow over her beloved's heart.

No time for that now, though. Integra had arrived, and there were plans for the day. The silk-slippered foot behind Tia's head started to tap impatiently, and Integra said, with obvious mirth in her voice, "Want me to leave you two lovebirds alone?" But as she said it, she extended a delicate hand to Tia who grabbed it and pulled herself up. Tenuen followed suit and then they were standing all together yelling, "Group hug!" The three were fast friends, with a great store of shared memories of fun, and the hug activated it all in a flash of joy.

Integra was almost as happy to have Tenuen home as Tia was, and it was hard to tell which of them was more excited about what was to come. Tia and Integra had planned a surprise for Tenuen, and they could hardly wait to get going. Tia gushed to Tenuen, "Just wait till you see what Integra has done!" and almost in unison Integra said with the same gleeful enthusiasm, "Wait till you see what Tia has done!" They were used to experiencing this kind of sweet synchronicity, since they shared so much in life. Laughing, Tia and Integra took Tenuen by his hands and started to lead him out of the garden. As the threesome set off walking, Integra impulsively stopped to hug Tenuen again. Grinning up at him she said, "Welcome back! Great to have you home!"

As happy as Tia felt in the moment, she still perceived a vague sliver of darkness. It was as if something had tainted the silver heart and soul she knew Tenuen to be. Intentionally shaking off these thoughts, she chose to focus on the excitement and fun of the moment.

CHAPTER 4
THE HEALING POD

The threesome stepped into the healing center and walked the long corridors, where the air smelled and tasted of salt from the canals of seawater flowing through the building. They were on their way to the laboratory that Tia and Integra shared. When they reached the lab, near the back of the building, they paused for a moment before a door that announced on a copper plaque: Vibrational Therapy Innovation Laboratory. Then they excitedly ushered Tenuen into the expansive room that had windows facing two directions. The view overlooked the tops of large willow trees that were just starting to bud, and Tia noticed that they looked like graceful yellow wings. The lab housed the first creation that Tia and Integra had completed together, and they could hardly wait to show it off to Tenuen.

Integra's expertise was in the utilization of the power of crystals. She captured the mystery, glory and capabilities of the crystals, and knew that knowledge had been infused into them during the centuries upon centuries of their growth within the earth. She understood that crystals chose when and how to reveal themselves and to share their qualities and power in order to serve and support the human experience. Integra tapped into the crystal consciousness and could create amazing things using these crystal allies. "Honestly," Tia often thought, "it's amazing what Integra can get stones to do." It was if some kind of magic was involved that Tia didn't understand, and when her talented friend created with crystals Tia would watch in fascination and wonderment.

For the present project, Integra had painstakingly selected crystals, mostly pink in color from the metal inclusions common to the area, and she pieced them together somewhat like a puzzle. She had pulverized some of the crystals into a powder, and then by adding a touch of selenium and some kind of clear sap she harvested (from where, Tia did not know), she had created a crystalline substance that could be poured into a mold, where it solidified into a new crystalline substance.

Tia was a master of the alchemy of precious metals, which also were gifts from the earth. In fact, she knew, metals were particular types of crystalline substances. She knew how to liquefy, mix, and cast these metals, creating anything she could form in her imagination.

The two friends had combined the knowledge, talents and ancient information that they each possessed in a synergy that culminated in the invention they had just completed. They had been industriously at work on it during the time of Tenuen's absence from the city, and now, it was ready.

Tenuen's eyes grew wide when they uncovered their invention —a healing pod.

Integra had created a vessel the size and shape of a bathtub out of a precise original crystal amalgam. Tia had fashioned a headrest, two handrests, and two foot-rests in the shape of indented bowls, out of a precise mix of silver, gold, and copper that formed an orichalcum that vibrated at a particular vibrational frequency. These were attached and integrated with the crystals in such a way that the healing pod seemed to be of one continuous piece. Thus, a person lying in the healing pod had contact through their head, hands, and feet with the orichalcum, while the rest of the body was in direct contact with the crystal amalgam.

The crystals sensed the vibrations of a person lying in the pod, reading where the body held imbalanced energy and needed calibration. The crystals and the orichalcum, together with the intentions for the treatment that had been set forth, tuned their vibration. The result was the manifestation of an ideal state of health for that particular body and mind. Sometimes it took two or even three sleeps for complete recovery, depending upon the state of dis-ease in the person, be it physical, mental, emotional, or spiritual. Tia and Integra had tested the pod, and so far, all cases had resulted in complete recoveries. Their test subjects had all exhibited the same general pattern. They would lie in the bed, and their aura would become visible, lighting up in a pattern of various colors that radiated out from the body in varying levels of intensity and brightness. As the person continued their treatment in the crystal bed, these patterns of light would become more orderly and the colors more evenly distributed around the body. Since this pattern had been so consistent, Tia and Integra assumed this would be what would happen with anyone who came to be tuned.

Tia and Integra explained to Tenuen that today the three of them were to finalize preparations for the pod to be opened to anyone seeking help. They planned to make it available to the general public the very next day.

As Tenuen walked slowly around the curious contraption, taking it in silently, Tia couldn't hide her pride and joy and blurted, "I don't believe you've ever been speechless before!" Integra and Tia beamed as Tenuen let out a low, long whistle. It was dawning on him that what he was witnessing was very important, perhaps even revolutionary.

Finding his voice again, Tenuen asked, "Can this really cure *any* state of imbalance?" The women sensed Tenuen's real question, and Integra motioned for him to get into the pod and get comfortable. She instructed him to set his intention and keep his focus on his desired outcome. Tenuen removed his shoes and then moved toward the pod, stopping momentarily to flash the women his best, most charming grin. Then in he went. Tia realized that this was the first time today that Tenuen had exhibited that boyish, carefree smile she so loved. Now that she'd seen it, she felt her heart warming, and she pulled her hands to her chest, intentionally holding that energy to her heart, and sending it throughout her body.

From inside the crystal bed, Tenuen smiled widely at the women again, placed his hands, feet and head into their holders, and closed his eyes. At the moment that Tenuen's extremities made contact with the crystals in the pod, Tia and Integra gasped, loudly and in unison.

They stood open mouthed and wide eyed, with eyebrows raised, staring in shocked disbelief at what was happening to Tenuen in the pod. Tia was silent, and "Oh!" was the only sound that Integra could manage to utter. What they were seeing happening to Tenuen as he lay in the healing crystal bed was completely different than anything they had seen so far. Light circles were spinning around his body like a helix. Countless streams of white light flowed out of his head like a fountain. That light poured down the front and back of his body and back into it through his feet. The constant flow of these streams of light encapsulated him in brilliant circles of every hue and color.

Tia turned slowly toward Integra and breathed ... "What's happening?"

CHAPTER 5
PERSEPHONE

The pyramid-shaped government building at the precise center of the capital housed all of the royal activities, and it was a busy place. Atlantis was the kind of open society where any citizen could receive an audience with someone in the royal court and expect their requests or issues to be considered.

The various positions Persephone occupied as a high priestess meant she spent quite a few hours there each week. As the kingdom's Master Teacher, she was responsible for the training of all teachers who taught the youth of Atlantis. In addition, as an especially trusted and valued confidant to Aztlan, Persephone served as a liaison between the king and the citizens who turned to him for help.

Persephone was educated in the Royal court, where she grew up alongside the ten Atlantean princes. She looked at King Aztlan as a sort of benevolent uncle, and he thought of her as fondly as he would a favored niece. She greatly cherished her shared history with the royal family, and considered it a pleasure and a high honor to serve the king by trying to make his life easier. The King knew that she would report to him anything truly needing his attention, and often Persephone was able to help the citizens herself. Only in rare instances, would she refer them to an audience directly with the king.

Arriving at her office on this glorious spring morning, Persephone prepared for the day ahead. She had a mirror in the corner of her light-filled office where she took a minute to brush off the leaves and dander that had attached to her royal blue garments on her way to work. Though she stood only five feet tall, Persephone carried herself with such ease and confidence and energy, that she gave one the impression of a large and commanding presence. Her short, straight, jet-black hair was cropped close to her small head, framing the delicate, chiseled features of her long, narrow face. Her green, almond shaped eyes were slightly slanted. Like Tia's and Integra's, her robes were in two layers, with embroidered symbols of educational achievements on the hem. Their royal blue color signified that she was a teacher as well as a high priestess.

Sitting at her desk, Persephone looked out the window at the glorious spring morning. She remembered having passed the garden wall of the healing center on her way to work, knowing that at that very moment her three closest friends were gathered to celebrate Tenuen's return home from the farthest reaches of the empire, as well as the new creation that Tia and Integra were launching. She closed her eyes momentarily and sent focused, loving energy to her friends. She was happy and excited for them, and even though she wished she could have joined them, sitting now in her office she knew she was where she needed to be that morning. She thought about how much she loved her life, and how fortunate she was to be able to work at things she was so passionate about. She would get together later with her friends. There was time enough for everything.

Taking a deep cleansing breath, she set to work preparing for the exciting class she would teach later that day. While she adored being a teacher of teachers, she also gave herself the opportunity to teach children directly now and then. She never wanted to give that up completely, so greatly did she enjoy it. Today, she planned to teach a group of teenagers how to sail a boat! She smiled at the thought of their earnest faces as they would absorb the new skill through her lesson, which would be delivered using meditational hypnosis.

CHAPTER 6
TARKUS DELIVERS HIS TRUTH AND PROPHECY

Engrossed in her lesson plan, Persephone was startled by sudden sharp knocking at her office door. It was her assistant, coming to inform her that a citizen from a far province had arrived and was requesting an audience with the king. Persephone told her to show the visitor into her office. A large man, almost as wide as he was tall, entered respectfully and introduced himself as Tarkus, a shepherd who had come with a message he thought worthy of passing on to the king.

Tarkus looked quite frightful, and his odor was not pleasant. His long messy gray hair matched an equally long gray beard, and from what Persephone could make out from the parts of his body visible around his dirty and unkempt garments, the rest of his body seemed covered with hair as well. As soon as he entered, he apologized for his appearance and condition, explaining that when at home, he spent most of his time with sheep and rarely saw other people. "I'm sorry Lady, I am not used to regular hygiene, and the long journey has only made things worse, I fear." Persephone nodded, and immediately asked the assistant to show him to the guest quarters, where he could avail himself of clean clothing, running water, and personal groomers who would help him bathe and dress.

"Thank you Lady Persephone, that is most kind."

While she waited for Tarkus to reappear, she applied herself once more to her work, and soon she was transported back to happy, focused thoughts of teaching and learning. When again she was interrupted by a knock on her door, the man before her looked quite transformed. Tarkus, clean and refreshed, entered her room. His mood, however, did not seem to have lifted. Persephone offered him a chair in front of the desk, and smiled at him. "How can I help?"

"Thank you, Lady Persephone," he said, "for taking the time to meet with me. For the short time that I have had the information I am going to give you, it has been a terrible burden upon me. I am thankful for your willingness to bear me witness."

Persephone smiled again at him, though a feeling of unease grew within her in response to Tarkus' obvious distress. "Of course," she encouraged, "I'm certain that what you have to say is important. Please go on."

"Well, Lady Persephone," Tarkus began, only to falter and become silent, twisting his handkerchief around and around in his hands. Seeing the trouble he was having getting the words out, Persephone did something she had learned years ago from one of her mentors. In her mind's eye she conjured the vision of a soothing shower of light and sent it to Tarkus using focused thought.

With that, he visibly relaxed, and began to speak. Hesitatingly, yet in a strong, clear voice, Tarkus began to let his story flow. He gave Persephone the impression of a simple and honest man who had no agenda and nothing to gain, but simply wanted to unburden himself.

Tarkus seemed greatly pained by what he needed to say. Trying unsuccessfully to conceal the shakiness in his voice, he cleared his throat again and again. Persephone leaned encouragingly toward him across her desk. "Do go on, please, Tarkus." There was a glass of water sitting in front of each of them, and Persephone slid his closer to him. He bobbed his head at her, murmuring "thank you," and gulped it all down in two swallows. With that, words began to tumble from him unimpeded, thought he took care to use precise language to convey his message.

Tarkus told Persephone what had happened two days prior. He had been with his grazing sheep in the mountain pasture in the high lakes area. As he shepherded the flock along the rocky shores of one of the lakes, he heard the desperate bleating of one of the ewes and realized that one of her lambs had gone missing. The ewe paced back and forth anxiously, and Tarkus listened carefully until he heard the lamb's mewing coming from high upon a rocky embankment. He started to climb up in hopes of rescuing it. "They are like my babies," he explained to Persephone. "I'm attached to all of them, and I even have names for each one. I keep them all together like a big family." Tarkus found the little lamb caught in some brambles on an escarpment, and scooping it into his arms, he started walking back down the steep incline toward the rest of the flock that was grazing close to the water's edge.

"That's when it happened, Lady Persephone. I'm not sure what to call it, exactly. A vision, perhaps? The surface of the lake showed me a picture. No, many pictures. It was a vision of a series of unfolding events that I was shown, as if they were just then happening." An expression of something between sadness and angst came over Tarkus' ruddy face, and after a pause, he said, "I'm sorry. I'll do my best, Lady Persephone, to recall the vision and tell you what the pictures showed me."

Persephone took a long, deep breath, and let it out very slowly. "No need to apologize, Tarkus. Take your time and tell me what you saw." Tarkus seemed to relax a bit, and started in again.

"First, I saw several people in a what looked like a laboratory. And I know
this doesn't make any sense, but they seemed to

be creating ... *beings*." Tarkus whispered that last word, and though Persephone was the only other person in the room, he looked around as if there might be someone who could overhear. "Those beings," he continued, "they were half human, and half horse." Tarkus continued to describe the events in his vision. He said the people who created the half horse and half human beings then whipped the beings, forcing them do something, though he couldn't tell what. Tarkus paused and shook his head, as if trying to free his mind from the vision of torture.

Persephone left briefly to bring more water for Tarkus, which he gratefully received and again downed all at once. Gathering himself for what he was about to relate, he looked at Persephone and said, "That was bad enough, but it was just the first part."

Persephone braced herself for the continuation of the story, and Tarkus' gaze seemed to go off into the distance as he recalled his vision. "It was the same people, in that laboratory," Tarkus lowered his gaze and continued. "They were making crystals, Lady Persephone! They had many sparkly wands that looked like the quartz that we mine from the earth. But the hands of people had made these crystals. They looked real, yet somehow they seemed strange and different." Persephone was fascinated and urged him to go on.

"Then I saw fires. Big cooking fires, with roaring flames that shot all the way up to the ceiling of the laboratory. The man-made crystals were put into those fires and they were engulfed completely by the flames. Through the flames I saw them glow with chaotic rainbow colors that grew brighter and brighter."

His voice got very low again, and his face took on an expression of fear. He pressed on. "In the next part of the vision, I saw the crystals again. This time they were in the sea, below the surface of the water, and the people who had made them were on the beach, watching and waiting. Suddenly there was a blinding flash. The crystals had all exploded, like bombs!" Tears rolled down the shepherd's cheeks, and he bowed his head. "Then I saw blood and carcasses and red muddy waters stretching for miles and miles. The explosions had caused the violent deaths of thousands of water creatures." Tarkus looked up and wiped the tears away from his face with the back of his hand.

Persephone knew how to keep her emotions in check and to maintain her emotional balance in times of duress. Her years of training in vibrational metaphysics had honed her skills at using her emotions as guidance. Her intuition was telling her that the shepherd's visions were important and that she should take notice and remember all the details. The feeling in the pit of her stomach felt like guidance telling her that this was not just the passing fancy of a shepherd wanting to spin a tale. It resonated as a message she was privileged to be entrusted with. She felt a solemn responsibility to try to understand.

Tarkus stopped talking and seemed to be grappling with internal discomfort. Persephone sensed that he had not yet revealed the entirety of his vision, and she waited patiently and focused on her breathing. The silence lingered. He seemed to be waiting for her to draw the rest of the vision out of him, so she urged, "Is there something more, Tarkus?" Resolving to continue, no matter how difficult, he said, "In the last part of the vision I saw balls of fire. Huge balls of fire. They rained furiously down on the city of Atlantis from the sky. People screamed and they ran searching for loved ones. Mothers, children, animals, homes - everything was bombarded and demolished by the balls of fire." There was another pause as Tarkus' eyes glazed over and he seemed to be seeing the vision again.

"And then," he continued quietly, "amidst the rubble and destruction, something else happened." Tarkus again lapsed into silence. "What happened?" Persephone urged him on, although she sensed it was something so big, something awful, something he wanted to unburden himself of by passing the vision on to her so as not to have to contain it anymore himself. She knew she had to hear it to the end, no matter how painful.

Tarkus seemed to be in a trance, and he spoke almost robotically as he delivered the final scene of the vision. "It was a wall of water. One impossibly gigantic wave. And then it was all over. Everything was gone." Tarkus looked directly at Persephone then, and the deep, penetrating sadness she saw in his eyes tore at her heart. She knew better than to let the sadness take hold in her, however, because then she could be of no help to Tarkus or anyone else.

Persephone rose from her chair and came around the desk to where Tarkus sat still, silent, and depleted. She put her hand on his arm, and out of a deep appreciation for what he had gone through to deliver his message, she thanked him sincerely. "Tarkus, your coming here was the right thing to do, and I commend you for the sacrifice and hardship you have endured to bring me this information. Is there anything else you want to share with me?" This last question was spoken as a habitual formality, and Persephone realized the irony as soon as she uttered the words. After all, there could be nothing to add after, "And then it was all over. Everything was gone."

"Would you like to rest before starting your journey back home? You may stay the night in the guest quarters where you were received." Tarkus, keeping his eyes downcast, bobbed his head gratefully. He knew the royal court often extended hospitality to citizens but had hardly dared to hope for an invitation. Upon hearing Persephone's soothing voice and kind offer, Tarkus felt that for the first time since seeing the vision two days previous, he could relax and allow himself a modicum of comfort. He started again to apologize to Persephone, "I'm sorry My Lady..." Persephone's hand was still on his arm, and she gave it a gentle squeeze, "Please don't be sorry, Tarkus. The fact that you made the journey here and shared your scrying with us may make all the difference for our beloved Atlantis."

Tarkus stood and began to let himself out. Just as he reached the great wooden door of the office, he turned back to Persephone.

"You called my vision a scrying? I hadn't thought of it that way, but I suppose that is what it was. I've never been involved with that sort of thing before."

Persephone watched him walk away, and then, sinking back into her chair, she began the process of bringing her thoughts about what she had just heard into alignment. Could it really be that she had just born witness to a prophecy of the destruction of all Atlantis? She shook her head and drummed her fingers on the table in front of her, trying to order her thoughts in such a way that she could make sense of the details of Tarkus' story.

"The art of scrying is a very advanced and complex art," she thought to herself. "Yet, the shepherd, Tarkus, seems to have had a spontaneous scrying experience." She sensed deeply that the Universe had used Tarkus as the medium to bring her a message, and that it was her job to give it consideration and use it correctly. She so much wanted to be able to dismiss Tarkus's vision as just the wild imagining of a shepherd who was perhaps looking for attention, or even slightly deranged. In her heart of hearts, however, she knew this wasn't so. It was clear to her that Tarkus had been a non-resistant and innocent receiver of the vision, and that he had executed his part perfectly. The next step lay with her.

So while Persephone considered the vision from every angle she could think of, a steady vibration of knowing kept bringing her back to the belief that the things Tarkus had been shown in his spontaneous scrying experience could actually be prophetic. As terrifying as it was to entertain, she knew they *could* truly constitute a warning or a prediction. "They might portend events to come," she thought. "Or they could be visions of events already taking place." She shivered at the thought. She didn't know which of these things, if either, was true, but Persephone knew better than to rely on her rational thought alone. Her inner knowing was just as reliable. Perhaps she would even need to alert the King. After all, it was her job to receive the populace and to listen to them and evaluate their offerings of information. She would not let herself pass this off as ridiculous, and shirk her duty to give it its due.

Of course thinking that the visions may have been scenes of actual events led to her vibration dipping in response to a tempest of emotions. Shock. Despair. Rage. Each emotion in turn took temporary hold of her as her thoughts skidded about and kept coming back to the worst possibility. "No," she told herself firmly. "Don't go there. Not now. My lifelong training in vibrational alignment will not desert me at this time. I won't let it."

Remembering that she had plans to meet her three closest friends later that day, Persephone took comfort in the thought of being able to share the burden of Tarkus's vision, and she knew they would help her make sense of it and decide what to do. It had been a long time since all four of the friends had been together, and she regretted that this would surely put a damper on their plans to celebrate Tenuen's return, but she knew she would not be able to keep it to herself, and that he, Tia, and Integra would not begrudge her asking for their help. There was nobody in the world whose perspective she valued more, and just knowing they would all soon be together brought profound relief and positive anticipation.

CHAPTER 7
SAILING LESSON

Persephone removed her gaze from the window and stood up and stretched. She took several deep cleansing breaths, and with each breath she whispered, "all is well." Then she focused firmly on the present moment and what needed to be done next.

There was plenty that needed attending to. It was time to leave if she didn't want to be late for class. The teenagers were probably already gathering in the learning center, excited for the lesson. They were going to learn the art of sailing small sea-going vessels. It was a rite of passage in Atlantis that every young person looked forward to achieving when he or she turned thirteen years of age. Boats were an important mode of transportation and recreation for the Atlanteans, and numerous vessels sailed among the bodies of land that made up the Kingdom. The children were used to being out on the water almost from birth. Being able to sail a small personal craft —one that could hold several passengers— was something that would make the youngsters more independent and more fully functioning members of society.

Persephone left her office, and putting all thoughts of the morning's interactions away for the time being, she started the short walk to the learning center. She was almost as excited as the teens themselves at the prospect of the sailing lesson. She always loved the feeling of accomplishment and satisfaction from seeing a group of students gain a new skill or some new knowledge. It was one of the great joys of her life to teach the Atlantean youth, and when a new class was due to learn to sail, or to play the traditional stringed instrument of Atlantis, she often reserved the opportunity to teach these classes herself.

As she walked along she purposefully put her attention on the things in the environment she could appreciate. The sunshine, and the way it glinted off the light-colored buildings. The bird-song and the far-away laughter of children. This helped take her focus away from the possibilities brought forth by what she had heard earlier. And she listened carefully for the everpresent beating of the drums of Atlantis. The drums could always be heard from everywhere in the city. Their reverberation was part of the heartbeat of the society, always beating out a constant rhythm. The drummers and the drums were non-physical and unseen, but their sound and vibration were ever-present backdrops to the physical day-to-day lives of the citizens. The drumming sounded louder or more faint according to the amount of focused attention the individual gave them. When listening intently to the drumbeat, one's heartbeat would entrain itself, to beat with the same rhythm, raising one's personal vibration to that of joy, health, and security.

Persephone walked, and she listened. And as her heartbeat matched the rhythm of the drums, she started to feel joyful anticipation, and there was a slight spring in her light footsteps as she made her way over the same sparkling, selenium-dusted footpath that her friend Tia had plied earlier that day. By the time she arrived at the learning center she was feeling aligned and balanced and ready to give the students her all as she led them through their lesson.

Persephone paused for a second in front of the heavy wooden door. Then she squared her shoulders, smiled widely, and pushed it open. The twenty students had already arrived, and were sprawled on comfortable cushions on the floor. The room was illuminated by daylight refracted through crystals that were set into the walls. Some of the crystals were as tall as the walls themselves. These were quartz crystals, with hexagonal facets, mined in the area and carved into prisms for the purpose of bringing light into the interior spaces of the buildings. The Atlanteans considered the crystals conscious beings with whom they had entered agreements to cocreate. They understood that the natural shapes in which the crystals grew gave them power to move and amplify energy. The crystals, for their part, held the intention to make themselves available to humans for use in bringing the light – both literally and figuratively.

The students greeted Persephone politely, and she crossed the room to her table and picked up a chime. By ringing it three times, she signaled the beginning of the teaching session.

Persephone instructed the students to lie back in fully reclined positions and make themselves comfortable. Teaching in Atlantis was done using the system of vibrational hypnosis that Persephone was master of and which she taught to all the teachers in the community. Vibrational hypnosis used the beat of the Drums of Atlantis to entrain the mind and heart. There was not a boat, nor even any water, in sight. Yet the students would soon emerge as skillful sailors, ready to man actual craft and sail out to sea with great skill and confidence.

Once they were situated and had closed their eyes, she instructed them to focus in on the sound of the drums. As they focused more and more intently, the drums seemed to beat more loudly. She reminded them to continue to listen only to the drums, and release any other thoughts or sounds. As they continued to do this, the students all entered a trance.

The drums continued their thump, boom-boom, thump. Persephone spoke softly, but her voice was heard clearly over the beating of the drums. She instructed the students to let go of conscious thought and when she felt they had all reached the most receptive state, she began to impart the skill of sailing to them. Her process had them become each element that is involved in sailing, until all of that understanding was synthesized into their very beings.

They became the harsh bite of a gale-force wind, and they became the gentle flit of a light breeze. They were the sun, the rain, the white-topped waves, and the gentle lapping water. Within this hypnotic reality, their beings expanded beyond their human physical selves.

"The conditions of the sea change around you," Persephone continued to guide them. "The tide ebbs and flows. The sea, in it's immense power and vastness, is now wholly within your being. You are everywhere the sea goes. You are licking the mountain ranges, and you are languishing on flat beaches. You contain infinite varieties of teeming life."

Tum-tum-tum, went the drums.

"You are the sails, the helm, the deck, and the ropes of the vessel. You are every board and nail in its hull. Love for the sea and all of what you have become fills your being, and you are complete in your appreciation for every aspect, large and small, of what it means to be a sailor."

Boom-de-tum-tum

"You are a sailor. You are a sure-footed and confident sailor, and you steer your craft with perfect expertise into open water, and back to safe harbor." With that, Persephone felt the lesson had ended. She now waited until she intuited that everyone had received all of the vibrational teaching, and that they were ready to come back to their everyday reality. She never tired of seeing the almost miraculous way the Atlantean method of teaching imparted knowledge and skills. She marveled to herself happily that the kingdom could now boast twenty more excellent sailors, having been given that part of what the collective human experience had gathered by the use of hypnotic meditation. She knew they would all soon set forth on actual boats on the water with no fear or hesitation.

She rang the chime three times again to signal the end of the lesson, and the teenagers came back to their regular consciousness, smiling and whispering to one another excitedly. When they got to their feet and left the learning center, each one stopped to thank Persephone and bid her goodbye. She thought about how much she loved the fact that Atlantis was such a polite and civil society.

Persephone always wrote an evaluation of each teaching session as soon as it was completed, so she took out a notebook and started to record some details about the how the lesson had gone. But almost immediately she stopped. A strong feeling came over her of being guided to go into a trance herself, where she would be given some kind of information. She knew from experience that she should do what she felt guided to do, so she sat back and focused on the drums. Almost immediately, she entered a deep trance.

CHAPTER 8
IN THE LABORATORY

Tia and Integra looked on as Tenuen's healing pod experience continued. His aura was behaving like a human-sized spinning torus. They could hardly believe their eyes. His body lay unmoving in the healing pod, but his energies were swirling in a dizzying array of colors and movement that held the women speechless with astonishment. Then, as quickly as it had begun, the spinning stopped, and Tenuen's aura became pink, then yellow, white, and gold. When it stabilized at a faint golden glow, they saw him begin to emerge slowly back into consciousness. He stretched his limbs, one by one, and shook his head from side to side. He opened his eyes, caught sight of his Tia and Integra, and grinned.

Tia realized she'd been holding her breath, and now she let it out in a whoosh, and smiled back at Tenuen, approaching him and giving him her hand as he eased himself out of the healing pod. "That was incredible. Absolutely astonishing! And just so... unexpected," she enthused. And Integra joined in, "It was powerful and beautiful! Now Tenuen, please tell us what you experienced, and we'll tell you what we saw happening."

Tenuen asked, "What do you mean? I was just lying there the

whole time. What could you have seen happening?" The women laughed and asked him whether he felt the healing pod experience had provided him with the expected healing or balancing of his energies. He nodded his affirmation, saying that it had far exceeded his expectations, and that he felt absolutely wonderful, energized, and balanced. He felt as if all of his bodily systems, as well as his emotional and mental systems, were fully functioning, easily, at their best.

Tenuen told Tia and Integra that as soon as he made contact with the orichalcum surfaces, he felt himself transported into the quantum field. Unlike his experience that morning with Tia, when they consciously intended to go into the field and had focused their minds and breath to facilitate it happening, in the healing pod Tenuen had simply been transported in an instant without even trying. "I don't know how you girls figured out how to do this, but this thing transports a person effortlessly into the non-physical realm." Tenuen beamed, partly because of the infusion of vitality the experience had provided, but also with the great pride and awe he felt that his betrothed and his friend had made such an amazing thing!

Integra offered her opinion as to why Tenuen's experience had differed so much from that of their other test subjects. "The pod reacts to the individual's vibration, and Tenuen's is already very much attuned to the non-physical dimension, so that he can go further and more deeply, as well as more quickly and easily into the state where his energy is at one with the light." She looked at Tia, who looked back at her, and in unison they said, "Well, the thing definitely works!!"

Feeling full of satisfaction at what had taken place, they declared themselves ready to make the healing pod available for the general public. But right now it was time to continue the celebration of Tenuen's homecoming. Their good friend Persephone was due to meet them later, and they all looked forward to having their group of four fast friends together once more, but first, Tia wanted Tenuen to herself again for a while. She told Integra, "We will see you when the sun begins to sink in the west, at Tenuen's office in the central pyramid."

The three friends left the lab, and the happy couple strolled toward the central garden area, where tucked into a particularly lush and secluded corner, was one of their favorite things—a hot mineral spring bath. A deep wooden tub had been fashioned to contain the waters from the spring and it always afforded a soothing, healing soak. The Atlanteans ascribed beneficial effects to this water that flowed from deep within the earth, and believed it to have therapeutic properties. Tia thought it would be the perfect spot for Tenuen to sit back, relax, and tell her all about his recent travels.

CHAPTER 9
TENUEN SPEAKS

Walking hand-in-hand, they smelled the magical spa area before it came into view. The tub was made of red cedar; its sweet scent tub wafted on the air and mingled with the fragrance of the many flowers and plants surrounding the hot spring, making them feel they were approaching a little piece of heaven. They stepped out of their robes, and climbed into the steaming, bubbling tub. Lying back on wooden slats a few inches under the water, they watched as long white clouds moved quickly through the sky on the brisk breeze. As they basked in the warmth and soothing comfort of the water, Tia snuggled under Tenuen's arm and turned toward him, laying her hand on his heart, just as she had done earlier on the grass in the garden.

Tia immediately felt a sudden change in her vibration. Just a moment beforehand, she had been completely immersed in a feeling of great wellbeing. Tenuen was home, the healing pod was ready and working really well, and all was right with her world. But now, with her hand registering the thump-thump of Tenuen's heartbeat, there again was that darkness, that shadow, that something that wasn't quite right. This time nothing interrupted her curious delving into what it might be. She knew she had to ask Tenuen what was wrong, even if it meant their sweet interlude at the spring might not be as positive and romantic as she had hoped.

"Tenuen, my love, are you troubled about something?"

He did not answer immediately, but when he turned and looked at her, she saw that his eyes had darkened. Tia felt the beginnings of some worry taking hold, but she focused on her knowing that whatever Tenuen was going to share was something she needed and wanted to learn. "We came here so that you could share your experiences with me. Please don't hold anything back," she said. "I am ready to hear it all."

Still lying back in the water, Tenuen's gaze went out past the clouds and the sun, and seemed to focus on nothing at all, or perhaps on his memories, so as to describe to Tia in perfect detail all that had happened on his trip. Tia was silent, knowing that he would deliver his story needing no prompting from her. She settled herself comfortably in the bubbling water, and listened.

"Well, when Father sent me on this trip, I assumed it would be like every other one I have taken in my job as Royal Ambassador. As you know, I was loath to leave you for what would be my longest journey yet, but because this particular assignment was to see my two eldest brothers, I was especially keen to accept it. Since my brothers have taken up their posts as governors of two of the farthest regions in the Kingdom, we don't spend that much time together anymore, and I wanted to catch up with their activities and their lives, in addition to finding out what I needed to report back to our father about the needs and well-being of their regions."

"So when I boarded Father's fastest ship for the thirty day journey, I was optimistic and looking forward to the experience. I didn't even mind that the distance was so great, because of my love of being out on the water. I expected the thirty days to pass enjoyably. Surprisingly, though, the trip proved to be utterly miserable. Almost as soon as we got out onto the open sea, I became seasick. I had never experienced this in all my years as a master sailor. I tried tea, meditation, and everything I could think of to balance my physical body and get relief. Nothing helped. I had to wonder if such an inauspicious beginning of my mission was a warning of sorts. I wouldn't turn back and disappoint my father, so I suffered for the duration of my journey, and I arrived at the port of my brother Azaroth's region feeling weak, out of sorts, and a bit confused."

Tenuen continued speaking, trying to keep his emotions in check. He clearly wanted to get the whole story out to Tia, and he spoke quickly and without much emotion at first. He related that when at last their vessel came to rest on the shores of Azaroth's region, he had stumbled up to the deck, fully expecting his brother to be waving from the shore, having come to meet him, since surely the ship would have been spotted as they came into port. But even after the vessel was tied to moorings and Tenuen and the crew were ready to disembark, there was no Azaroth, no carriage, no welcoming fanfare, nothing. Tenuen was disappointed, and his crew was confused. Nobody at all had come to greet a ship of the Royal Court? The Prince's surprised attendants bade him return to his quarters to rest while they set out to alert Azaroth of his brother's arrival.

Tenuen retired to his berth and told himself it would not be long, and that all was well. Surely his brother had been detained and would arrive soon. He grew even more confused, however, when later it was Sipho who came to collect him and take him to Azaroth. Tenuen was happy to see Sipho, a childhood friend now in Azaroth's employ as a trusted assistant. However, his happiness was short-lived, because Sipho behaved quite strangely. He seemed uncomfortable rather than pleased at seeing Tenuen. He was perfunctory and proper as he transported his old friend from the ship and delivered him to his brother, but there was little warmth in their interaction.

"Sipho seemed shut down. Strained, somehow. He wouldn't make eye contact with me," Tenuen related to Tia, who kept silent but was becoming more curious by the moment. "What in the world...?" she wondered. The thought occurred to Tia that Sipho must have been withholding a secret. What else could explain such behavior on his part? Everyone in the royal court held Sipho and his family in high esteem, but she knew that Sipho was particularly loyal to Azaroth. "Go on, please," she encouraged Tenuen, and as he steadied himself to continue, she looked around at their beautiful surroundings in an effort to stay in the vibration of appreciation, helping her to keep herself balanced, loving and receptive.

Sipho had driven Tenuen in a carriage to Azaroth's dwelling place. Since Tenuen's last visit, Azaroth had moved to a large and lavish palace, much different than the modest home he had lived in before. Tenuen noticed much hustle and bustle around the castle as a staff of what looked like hundreds worked on the grounds and around the buildings.

Tenuen described to Tia how his brother met him at the palace, after Sipho led him through an impressive entrance made of orichalcum and pure gold. "Our initial meeting was as you might expect," he told her. "My brother embraced me and seemed pleased that I had come, and our brotherly relationship seemed intact and familiar. I soon began to feel a new and unfamiliar element, however. I perceived a distance, or... a lack of trust and openness in the way Azaroth spoke to me. He seemed tired and stressed, and his eyes darted around and could not seem to come to rest. I assumed that since it had been more than fifty moons since our last meeting, perhaps we just needed to warm to one another again. We talked about family matters, and I told Azaroth about the upcoming nuptials you and I will celebrate and he expressed delight for us. Then, when it seemed we had dispensed with the personal and family news, I decided to turn to the business at hand. After all, I had been sent on a mission—to assess the activities of his region—and I intended to complete that mission."

Tenuen's usual style of talking, especially when sharing things with Tia, was lighthearted. Tia was very aware that this story was being related in an entirely different cadence and emotional tenor than she was used to coming from him. His speaking was alternately halting, as if he couldn't quite find the words, and rushed, as if he wanted to get done as quickly as possible with the sound of these implausible events coming through his lips.

Sensing that he needed space to gather his thoughts, Tia shifted her body and sat up at a very slight distance away from Tenuen, and she removed her hand from his heart. He looked again off into the far distance beyond the sun.

Being back home now, with Tia, in this idyllic natural pool, the things Tenuen had observed on his trip almost seemed like they had happened in a dream, and he was sorely tempted to leave them in the realm of "impossible", and go on with his life in his beloved Atlantis. He knew, however, that he had to face whatever reactions would be elicited from Tia and, ultimately others, by telling the truth, as difficult as that would be.

"I asked Azaroth for a tour of his community and his operations. I could tell he was hesitant, which I found confusing. Why would he not be proud to show his brother, who would report to our father, all that he was accomplishing in his region?" While they ate the hearty meal traditionally served when visitors came, Tenuen repeated his desire to be taken around so he could begin to gather information for his report. Azaroth finally relented, of course, and they left the palace with an entourage, including the now sullen Sipho and several of Azaroth's high-ranking ministers.

The first stop on the tour was a large expanse of land that had been stripped by mining. Recalling the scene, Tenuen paled, and he looked at Tia. "Gold," he whispered, and swallowed hard. Then finding his voice again he repeated, "Gold. They are mining gold at the fastest rate ever accomplished anywhere in the kingdom." Tenuen went on to say that the way they had accomplished an increase in the speed and efficiency of obtaining gold from the earth was shocking and upsetting. He asked Tia to prepare herself to hear it.

Tia looked at him with an open expression, ready to hear anything, but not understanding how mining gold, which was the basis for the Atlantean economy, could be a bad thing. After all, gold was one of the elements in orichalcum—the precious substance that was so important in the construction of the healing pod. All of this went through Tia's mind as she listened to Tenuen's description of the large, efficient, and productive gold mines in his brother's region. Tenuen continued. "At first, it seemed very impressive. I assumed my brother was mining gold to be shared throughout the kingdom, and my reaction was positive. But soon it became clear that I had been mistaken about his motives."

"The truth is," Tenuen sighed, "he is stockpiling gold in order to use it for power and control. Power and control over the entire kingdom. Power and control over men, women, and beasts. I could hear in his voice and see in his eyes that he has forgotten all the teachings we grew up steeped in. He seems to have forgotten the awesome power of the illusion, and has started to believe in the illusion of power. He was so different, not at all like the brother I remembered so well. His values have shifted. The same is true of my brother Carturrah. But, I am getting ahead of myself..."

Tia didn't know what to say, it was all so unexpected and unbelievable, and so she just continued to listen. "That wasn't the worst part," Tenuen went on. "My brother's seemingly insatiable desire for more gold, and therefore more power, made him impatient with the pace of the mining. He wanted a way to make it go even faster. I know this sounds incredible, and I would not have believed it had I not seen it with my own eyes, but, Azaroth has created... through genetic manipulation done by the most prized scientists of his region—a new species of creature."

Now Tia was sitting bolt upright. This was sounding far-fetched. She knew perfectly well, however, that Tenuen would only be telling her, with complete honesty and simplicity, exactly what he observed.

There was more. "This creature was created for the express purpose of being his slaves." Tenuen went on to explain that Azaroth had commissioned the finest medical minds of Atlantis to use genetic mutations to bring about the creation of this slave species called centaurians, whose members were half horse and half human. Azaroth had reasoned that the human half would be able to use a pick-axe with the necessary precision to mine the ore, while the horse's limbs and back provided the extra brawn and strength needed to increase stamina and output. Tenuen explained that Azaroth and his scientists had succeeded at bringing the new creature into existence, but that while they would not admit it, some of their expectations as to the behavior of the centaurians had apparently fallen short. It seemed that Azaroth had assumed they would be compliant and obedient worker-beasts, much as he would expect from a horse, doing exactly his bidding without rest or rebellion. He had not bargained for the fact that the human element caused the centaurians not to take easily to being captive against their will and kept in slavery.

As Tenuen continued to describe the situation at his brother's gold mines, his eyes grew wild and his voice louder. "I observed a sad lot of beings— hundreds of them, perhaps even thousands— forced to work night and day to enrich my brother's coffers," he lamented. "Azaroth employs military troops that don't spare the whip to keep the centaurians hard at work in the mines. They are expected to work to the exclusion of anything else. They stop once a day for a meal, and at night they sleep only four hours. As exhausted as they are, they keep working, out of fear."

Tia pushed herself out of the water and sat on the side of the tub behind Tenuen. The sun's rays were warm on her body, drying her, and on any other day she would have basked in their light, but now, she felt an odd chill, and donned her robes. Tenuen, still lying back in the water, kept talking. It seemed to be getting easier for him as he went along.

"The speed and process of the gold mining are having other consequences as well. They are causing a strip of land close to the sea to erode, and a toxic muddy sludge is being created which Azaroth's workers are discarding into the sea. The fishermen of the region are having to move much farther into the open ocean than they ever have before to find live, healthy fish." Tenuen continued, painting a picture with his words the sludge driving away not just the fish, but also all of the other sea creatures that had lived near the shore. Tenuen wasn't sure if Azaroth had made it clear they were no longer welcome, or whether the effects of the mining had made it impossible for them to get to shore. "Azaroth didn't actually seem to care, one way or another."

As he spoke, Tia saw that Tenuen was close to tears, but holding himself back from actual weeping. She felt her own sadness well up, yet she remained quiet and waited for him to continue.

Tenuen turned himself around in the water, and putting his elbows on the side of the tub, he looked up at Tia. "I had to marshal all the skills I have practiced all my life in order to stay aligned with my purpose while I observed all of what I'm describing to you. I have all of our teachers to thank for that. As the tour went on, and Azaroth warmed to talking to me and giving me this glimpse of the truth of what was going on there, I showed interest and yes, even appreciation, for his cleverness. Knowing my brother like I do, I used the fact that he thinks he controls me, and his desire to boast, to my advantage. I would not allow him to discern the shock, disbelief, and fear that would surely take over my emotional state had I allowed myself to focus on the horrific truths of what I was observing. I knew I needed to placate him for now, and to keep my emotions in check. My first priority was to gather as much information as I could."

When he had seen enough of Azaroth's operations to complete

his report to the king, he rested in the palace for a few weeks trying to regain his equilibrium after being shown such unexpected goings on. Then he requested of his men that they sail his ship to Carturrah's port, while he and several attendants crossed the border between the two brothers' regions on foot.

"When I said good-bye to Azaroth, I had a strange premonition that I would not lay eyes on my eldest brother, or on Sipho, or anyone else in this region, again in this lifetime. Azaroth's eyes seemed full of ambivalence when he saw me off, though he offered parting gifts and said the customary blessings over my travels. His eyes seemed to beseech me, but it wasn't clear what he wished me to say or do. Even as he embraced me and bade me safe travels, we both felt a combination of relief and regret."

"During the weeks that I and my entourage walked toward the land of my brother Carturrah, I marveled at the beauty of the landscape, and how peaceful everything seemed. I was able calibrate my emotions to match that peace, in spite of the starkly contrasting events and sights I'd just left behind."

Tenuen continued his story, recounting how when he'd arrived in the region that was governed by Carturrah, he was greatly looking forward to being able to talk to him about what was going on with their eldest brother. Surely, he assumed, Carturrah knew nothing of Azaroth's sinister and even evil behavior. Had he known, Tenuen had reasoned, Carturrah would have tried to intervene, or reported to their father long ago. "The prospect of having someone with whom to discuss all I'd found out made me pick up the pace as my party approached Carturrah's dwelling place."

Tenuen stretched out his limbs in the water, and readied himself to deliver the next part of the story. Turning to face Tia again, he reached his hand out of the water and rested it on her knee. She held her breath while she waited for him to continue, hoping against hope that Carturrah had indeed helped him, or at least reassured him in some way. Removing his hand, and reclining again in water, Tenuen narrowed his eyes, but kept them open, as he continued his story. His voice became low and Tia had to lean forward to hear.

"He was crazy, Tia," he said softly. "I barely recognized Carturrah. Save for his physical appearance he was nothing like the brother I grew up with and thought I knew better than anyone." Tenuen spoke with resignation, shaking his head slowly. "It is as if both he and Azaroth have fallen under some kind of spell."

"At first, Carturrah greeted me with what seemed like genuine happiness, and we exchanged compliments and joked that we had both remained quite handsome. The laughter and banter didn't last, though. Very shortly after I arrived, I began to see signs of some kind of craziness in Carturrah's eyes, in his movements, and most of all, in the things he said. Once the madness—yes, I'll call it that—started coming out, Carturrah wasn't really able to hold it at bay. He began to talk to me in an agitated and excited voice, using wild gestures. In my worst nightmares I could not have imagined and would never have thought possible the things he shared about what is happening in his region, under his direction. What he revealed was even more shocking than what Azaroth had shown me."

"After the welcome feast, Carturrah immediately took me to a laboratory that is hidden deep in a huge underground cavern. We had to pass rows and rows of military guards in order to gain entry. When we got to the lab, he became even more agitated, and he seemed to allow any remaining mental shackles to come off his madness. He appeared to be quite unhinged with the lust of power and the quest for more. It was so strange to hear my brother sounding for all the world as if he had come to believe wholeheartedly in the illusion of power."

There in Carturrah's underground laboratory, Tenuen had lost his last vestige of hope that his brother would be an ally who would help to undo the terrible damage Azaroth was wreaking on his corner of the kingdom. It was here that Tenuen came to understand the depth and breadth of what was taking place, and that Carturrah was just as deeply involved in these dark activities, if not more so, than Azaroth.

"Carturrah had brought me to this place to show me just what he was doing toward the quest for power, and how he meant to attain it. It turned out that he and Azaroth have been working together for quite some time, formulating a sinister plan, based not on the truths we were taught all our lives, but rather, based on what they think they know..."

Tenuen took a breath and after a moment he started again, speaking a little more slowly and quietly. "Tia," he said, "my brother *knows* that only by mastering the power of illusion do we create our reality. As a young man he was always excited by this knowledge. He understood completely that the illusion of power is false. But now..."

Turning to look at Tia again, Tenuen saw that she seemed to be deep in thought, trying to make some semblance of sense out of what he'd said, but trying not to react until he finished his story. He waited for her to make eye contact, and when her gaze remained far away, he gently touched her knee again. His touch brought her back into bodily awareness, and she was momentarily dazed.

"This next part may be the hardest for you to hear," he said gently, looking straight into her eyes. "It is about the crystals." Tenuen knew how Tia revered the crystals that were brought forth lovingly from the earth, and it pained him to know the horror she would feel at what he was about to reveal. She swallowed, took a deep breath, and looking into Tenuen's eyes she said, "Please. Tell me about the crystals."

Tenuen's whole body seemed to sag inward. He closed his eyes slightly as if trying to look into the past. He described the laboratory and the people working in it, most of them learned scientists, as well as some apprentices and laborers. At first glance, the lab had seemed to be a glittery, magical place, because it contained piles and piles of quartz crystals. When he first entered the space, Tenuen had gasped with delight to see so many crystals in one place. However, then he had to wonder how there came to be so many, and his mind jumped immediately to the possibility that Carturrah had found a way to mine quartz more efficiently, the way their brother was mining gold.

"With that thought, my heart sank," he said quietly to Tia. "And I braced myself against finding out that Carturrah had brought forth a race of slaves to bring more crystals out of the ground. But, as we toured the facility, I became even more confused. The crystals here were all very large, and they had no imperfections in clarity or form. Never have I seen crystals emerge from the earth with such uniform size and shape."

"Wait until Integra hears about this," breathed Tia. "She'll want to travel straightaway to the region of Carturrah!"

"No. No, Tia please let me finish."

Tenuen continued his account, telling Tia that Carturrah's face lit up when he saw Tenuen's confusion upon examining the crystals. He excitedly told Tenuen to look around at what the scientists in the lab were actually doing. Tenuen stepped up to one of the tables and ran his hand along a row of visually stunning wands that were as long as his arm. These crystals had the same hexagonal structure as the quartz he was familiar with. Their clarity was undisturbed by inclusions, and they refracted the light from the fires the scientists used to illuminate their work, sending rainbows onto the walls of the laboratory. But when he touched the facets of the crystals, they seemed to vibrate with a strange and unfamiliar resonance.

"All at once, understanding rushed into my mind. The people working in this place were not working *with* crystals. They were manufacturing them! These specimens were not brought out from the ground by some special mining process. They were not created inside the earth over millions of years. They were made in that very room, by the hands of humans. These crystal allies were not voluntarily and joyfully co-creating with Carturrah and his people. They were—like the centaurians in the land of our older brother—slaves to the desire for power. These crystals existed to do the bidding of the humans who created them."

"When this understanding came over me," Tenuen continued, "I stood very still and commanded myself to come into alignment so that I could continue to function, and not alarm my brother with my shock and disbelief. Forcing myself to keep respect and curiosity in my voice, I asked Carturrah why he was manufacturing these crystals."

At this point in the story, Tia felt herself starting to shiver, and she sloughed off her garments and slipped back into the warm water. She took both of Tenuen's hands in hers. They sat still for several moments. Tia's thoughts were reeling. Man-made crystals? How could such a thing be possible? What kind of consciousness could such a crystal possess? It sounded as if in the manufacturing process these crystals were being infused with an intention to harm! She looked around her at the buildings that surrounded the hot spring, and mused at how Atlanteans used their crystal allies to bring light and joy, and how the quartz crystals, similarly to the metals in the orichalcum, which were also crystalline in nature, raised the vibration of each of their homes and other structures. Tia put her focus there momentarily, as she reached for her always present underlying knowing of well-being. From where she lay in the pool with Tenuen, she saw the city towers that rose around her. The supporting columns were painted primarily red, with black bases, and they stood out in bold relief against the white stone that made up the main parts of the buildings. She marveled at how the city's architects worked in partnership with the crystals, installing them into the walls of all the buildings in such a way that they reflected and refracted any light that was available. The eternal knowing of well-being, which is built into the very fabric of life itself, flowed through and around the crystals. When the moon was new, the starlight would glow through the crystals. And when the moon was full, the crystals would help it cast a wonderful bright shine over everything. As she tried to relax again in the water, everything in her visual field held something whose beauty was magnified by natural crystals that were gifts from the earth.

Tia brought her attention back to the immediate surroundings. It all seemed surreal to her. How could she be sitting here, with the man she loved, in this beautiful place, in the loveliest of moments, and yet be hearing the most horrific news imaginable?

"What was his answer?" she asked. "Why would Carturrah want man-made crystals when Earth is so generous with the crystals it forms over millions of years within its depths?"

"He did not answer me directly, but it was clear to me that Carturrah and Azaroth are using these human-produced crystals to further their grab for power. Carturrah ordered his scientists to develop them, and he oversees the production and testing. The manufactured crystals have no free will. They are not asked whether they choose to co-create with my brothers and to be instrumental in their plans. These crystals are used to store up energy from the sun. I'm not sure what their process is for accomplishing this, but they have been able to get these crystals to collect much energy in such a way that when they are detonated they give off a force greater than any explosive yet known. Carturrah has been having these explosive crystals tested in the ocean, and so far they have been able to keep it secret from other humans because the explosions are underwater. But the water creatures see and know, and they suffer and die. This testing has resulted in the destruction of much of the underwater landscape, and so very many of the water-dwelling creatures have perished as a result."

Tenuen seemed to have talked himself out. He slowly climbed out of the pool, but it seemed too much effort to stand, so he simply lay on the grass and looked up at the sky. The sun was beginning to sink behind the tallest buildings, and there were shadows in their corner of the garden which just moments earlier had been illuminated with bright sunshine. The birds ceased their chirping and the butterflies that had been flitting about stayed still, perched on flowers. It was as if all the creatures, and even the air, participated in the shock of what Tenuen was relating.

Tia too came out of the water, and fastened her robes close to her body in an effort to ward off a chill that suddenly penetrated to her very bones. Her face remained impassive, but she was grappling with a great inner turmoil. Tenuen's brothers were like brothers to her as well. It was difficult to believe what she had heard—that they had undergone such a complete transformation of character in their time away from the city. It was difficult for her to rein in her feelings as they skidded from one emotion to another. She felt something like despair, but it alternated with hope because she kept bringing herself back to the knowing that no matter what, everything that happened was for the good.

Tenuen just seemed tired. It was as if all of the confusion and anger he'd felt since he first set foot in his brothers' regions had drained out of him, leaving him empty and with no real wherewithal to try to make sense of anything or to go on from there. He'd been waiting, holding himself together, until he could tell Tia everything. His happiness at their reunion that morning had been genuine, but he'd had to put the events of his trip firmly away temporarily. Now that he had spoken about what he'd seen, it all seemed more real. Yet at the same time, he felt more detached from it, since, momentarily at least, having shared the burden was giving him a modicum of relief.

The silence between them lasted several minutes, until at last Tia rose to her feet, looked down at Tenuen and sighed. "We must go and meet the others, my love." Her voice sounded strange to Tenuen; as if she had grown much older in just the time they had been at the hot spring. He nodded as he raised himself to a sitting position and dressed silently.

CHAPTER 10
FOUR FRIENDS REUNION

When they arrived at the Central Pyramid, on their way to meet their friends in Tenuen's private chambers, Tia and Tenuen stopped for a short audience with King Aztlan. There was a brief but very warm exchange of greetings between father and son, and then the king waved them on to meet Persephone and Integra, saying there was time enough for Tenuen to give him his full report in the coming days. The couple continued through the halls of the pyramid and entered the inner sanctum, where they pushed open one of the arched wooden doors and entered Tenuen's office. It was an opulent yet cozy and inviting space full of hand-woven carpets and ornate furniture. Food and drink had been laid out for them to enjoy.

Tia tried her best to do what Tenuen had done earlier, and purposefully put her feelings about what she had heard aside so that the four friends could be joyous and unencumbered at least for a time. She was very conflicted, however, because she also wanted very much to quickly bring the other two into the knowledge of what Tenuen had seen. The urgency and the utter magnitude of it all were at odds with her usual preference for lighthearted gatherings.

Persephone and Integra arrived within moments of one another and everyone hugged everyone else at least twice before they settled down, grinning at one another. Tia couldn't wait another moment, though, and when the other women saw her smile disappear, they understood that something was afoot and gave her their attention.

"As much as we wish this could just be a friendly gathering after such a long time, we must use this as an urgent meeting and share something important with you both," said Tia in what she hoped was a normal, even voice. Tenuen signaled Tia with his eyes that he should be the one to tell their friends, and she nodded.

As Persephone made herself comfortable on a chair, she announced, "I too have something important to share, and will need input from all of you before I go to the King with the information."

As Tenuen took a seat facing the three women, he looked into each of their much-loved faces in turn and he showered them with soothing energy from his mind's eye. Then he began. For the second time that day, he related all of the details of the saga of his trip, and this time the horror was no less deeply felt in the depths of his heart. Hearing his own words aloud again only made it all the more frightening. And Tia, having heard it all just a scant hour before, felt it just as acutely this time as before. There was no denying any of it now. No turning away. She felt that lifetimes had elapsed since her meeting with Tenuen in the garden that morning.

As Tenuen spoke, Tia watched the faces of her two friends change rapidly from open and calmly curious, to utterly incredulous. At first, neither Integra nor Persephone made any movement or sound as they listened, save for their subtly changing facial expressions. When Tenuen reached the part of the story that pertained to the crystals, however, Integra jumped to her feet, and began to pace back and forth across the room, her crimson robes swinging as her steps hit the floor, increasing in speed and force each time she turned. Her face registered shock, disbelief, sadness, and then, anger. "They know better!" she shouted. "Tinkering with the powers of crystals, with bad intent!" Integra grew pale with her fury, and sweat broke out on her brow. In a flash of purple, Tia was up and at her side. She didn't reach out to touch Integra, knowing that is not what her dear friend would want just now. She paced with her a few steps, and when Integra stopped and stood still, Tia stood next to her, trying to provide a stable vibration by breathing slowly in and out, and as she did so, she focused her loving energy on Integra using her eyes. Integra responded, slowed her own breathing, and looked back at Tia with gratitude. All the while, Tenuen continued to speak clearly and without hesitation, wanting them to hear it all through to the end.

Persephone, still seated, had an inscrutable expression on her face as she kept listening intently, hanging on Tenuen's every word. She nodded sagely at intervals, as if validating what Tenuen was saying. Tia found this curious and somehow unnerving.

CHAPTER II
PERSEPHONE DELIVERS HER TRUTH AND PROPHECY

After Tenuen described the exploding crystals and the deaths of the many sea creatures, Persephone finally uttered a sound. It was a sob of deep and profound sadness. The others turned toward her, but she kept her eyes on Tenuen, and wiped away a tear. Tenuen indicated that he had finished, and that Persephone should say what was on her mind.

Nobody could have expected anything like what she told them next. As she shared what the shepherd, Tarkus, who had come to see her that very morning, had seen in a spontaneous scrying vision, the collective thought in the room became, "this is even worse than we imagined just moments ago..." Many of the elements of Tarkus's scrying vision were almost identical to what Tenuen had actually seen happening!

The four friends were among the most educated of the citizens of Atlantis. A prince and three priestesses—all steeped in the knowledge of how to maintain vibrational alignment. All expertly trained in focusing energy in the direction of what they wanted to create. And yet, each and every one was finding it difficult to maintain steady breathing and not to careen out of emotional control. This was simply unfathomable information. Almost completely incredible. They all knew that it was no accident that Tarkus had appeared before Persephone on the very day that Tenuen was to come back to the city and relate what he had seen. They all now knew, with each experience confirming and informing the other, that they had been tasked by the Universe with deciding, and guiding, the next steps for Atlantis.

And as unbelievable as all of this was, at this point there was still more— and only Persephone knew. She alone at this moment grasped the complete enormity of what Tarkus and Tenuen had seen. She allowed them a few moments of steady breathing before she spoke quietly. "I have more to relate to you, my friends." They all looked at her with surprise. What more could there possibly be? Persephone explained that after her visit with Tarkus, she had taught her class as usual, and that directly afterward had felt guided to go into trance during which she received information from the non-physical realm.

"My spiritual guides gave me many details which now that I have heard Tenuen's firsthand report, come into the bright light of truth and clarity, I will share it all with you now."

Persephone had everyone's full attention as she explained that while in the trance she had been shown that the entire Kingdom of Atlantis was already overshadowed by something dark, something ominous. She reiterated that already there was not a corner of the kingdom left unaffected. Then, while the others were still absorbing that, she went on to describe the final scene in Tarkus's vision—the fireballs raining down on Atlantis, bringing about its ultimate, complete destruction.

The messages Persephone had received in her trance that morning were further confirmation that the information was real, but they realized that it made clear the frightening additional possibility that the destruction of Atlantis could actually be imminent, and not just a distant possibility.

Darkness had fallen by that time, but not one of the four friends rallied to light a lamp or set out a fire, and all of Tenuen's attendants had been instructed that their meeting was private. They sat in the shadows and tried, yet again, to accomplish the almost impossible task of regaining equilibrium and trying to internalize the likelihood that their entire civilization was doomed to complete and utter destruction.

It was not long after the entirety of the horror hit them, however, that all four began their inner recovery. Always before, when one of the friends was unhappy about something, they would support one another by saying things they knew to be true, such as "questions are always accompanied by answers," and "All is always well," and "Things happen for a reason." This time, though, the usual platitudes, even though perfectly true, just didn't seem adequate for the enormity of the upset. Tia tried. "Okay, everyone, let's try to keep our thoughts general. Don't think about the specific details of what we've learned. Try to think general truths that feel better." Integra tried to give her reinforcement. "We understand, after all, that all beings are eternal! There is no real death. We know that all is well, even when appearances and circumstances seem most definitely to be to the contrary." Tenuen and Persephone didn't argue, but neither did they join in the verbal efforts. All four kept reordering their thoughts and focusing on those general truths until their panic subsided somewhat.

Finally registering the fact that night had fallen, Tenuen, Tia, and Integra started again to move about. Tenuen called for refreshments and for a fire be laid to bring light and warmth into the room. When the food arrived, Tenuen's attendant, upon seeing and feeling the somber mood of the group of friends, looked questioningly at the prince. When no explanation was forthcoming, he left quietly and discreetly, promising to check later to see if they needed anything more.

Tia again spoke first. "It would clearly be folly to disregard everything we have seen and heard today. The synchronicity seems to point to validation, and it seems that we must accept the inevitability of it. We must take steps to preserve that which is good in our kingdom, while we still can. And, since we have this foreknowledge, perhaps it will allow us to save..."

"No." Persephone interjected. She had remained seated and seemed to be deep in thought, but at Tia's last words she rallied and responded sadly, "No. That is not to be, my friend." Then to the group at large she added, "I'm sorry, but there is yet more information, and you all need to hear it right away. There was more to my trance meditation earlier today. I will go back into the trance and from that connection to Infinite Intelligence, I will tell you the rest. I promise after I tell you these final things, you will know all that I do."

Persephone's eyes became unfocused, and she began to speak methodically, with a slightly different inflection and tone than were usual for her. She spoke dispassionately, in a flat monotone, not stopping for thought, but simply pouring forth the rest of the message.

There is a thing, some kind of infection, if you will, that is embodied by certain people, all over the Kingdom of Atlantis, who have become the "Children of the Darkness." This phenomenon is much larger and more widespread than what Tenuen witnessed. In addition to what is happening in the regions overseen by his brothers, every other part of Atlantis has been similarly affected by this darkness. While our Atlantean integrity is still strong in many people and creatures, the civilization as a whole has become divided and collectively is now a match to something baser, something of a much lower vibration. Thus, our many years of thriving will now come to an end. I will describe to you now the actions we four friends are being called upon to take at this juncture. Although the entirety of our beloved Atlantis is going to be destroyed because its dominant vibration has become unsustainable, we are entrusted with preserving all that is good in this civilization.

We are to create a large stone labyrinth, which will be walked by all those who are drawn to it in coming generations, far in the distant future. This labyrinth will be the key to resurrecting the knowledge of Atlantis.

Integra, you must help us choose powerful crystals, which are to be buried at regular intervals in the labyrinth. Each crystal will be infused with a piece of the information that our Atlantean society has come to know about how the Universe works. The crystals will store the sum total of what Atlantis has achieved and all that we have learned during our Kingdom's existence. They will be the keepers of the knowledge of the rise and fall of cycles of human civilizations. The present cycle is ending, but a new one is beginning. Life is eternal. There will be many cycles, until one day, far into future earth-time, in a place that will be known as America, the very last cycle of darkness to befall humanity will be transformed by people who will be born with the express purpose of bringing the light of good, once and for all.

When that time comes, because a large enough number of people will be living at the high vibration necessary for the human species to be ready to continue its evolution into ever-expanding states of consciousness, humans will no longer have to dip into the lower vibrating regions of experience. No longer will it be necessary to explore the depths of darkness in order to experience the light. Contrast will no longer need to be as pronounced. These new humans will live in accord with nature, in peace, creativity, and expansion. In this new era, in this new mass vibration, Atlantis will rise again, and will be stable for millions of years thereafter. This time, Atlantis will provide a place where humans can thrive, living in grace and gratitude, while having endless exciting adventures both in consciousness and in physicality.

Those who are to herald the beginning of this new age will be attracted to the labyrinth. When they find it, they will walk its paths, and at each turn, as they pass the buried crystals, they will be drawn into meditation, through which information from Atlantis will become integrated into their knowledge. Their vibration will be upgraded with each crystal they pass. By walking the labyrinth, these future humans will tap into a newly evolved way of being, where they access all that is known now, here, in Atlantis.

Yes, we are going to be forced to give up the land we have loved so much, but we have been privileged to have lived here, and we are similarly privileged to be able to impart to future generations and to other areas of the world, the knowledge of how humans can thrive, in all ways, on the physical plane.

Persephone said all this without stopping for breath. Now her breathing came back to normal and she came out of her trance. Her eyes narrowed and she looked around at her friends. All of them were crying, tears falling soundlessly as they allowed their feelings to flow along the emotional scale, starting with utter powerlessness and fear, and slowly climbing to anger, denial, and almost, almost, reaching acceptance. They couldn't really touch that yet, but they knew they would in time. Meanwhile, they knew from what Persephone had just told them, that making a plan for next steps could not be delayed.

Tia said, "Friends, I propose that we consult with Mira the Stargazer to find out if she can tell us how much time we have left. Knowing the timeline will help us assess the urgency of our actions. Tenuen, if you agree, I will then go to King Aztlan with you, to present what we know to him. Presumably, he will want to alert the populace so that citizens who want to leave Atlantis to save themselves will be able to relocate in time, hopefully causing as little panic as possible in the kingdom. Intentional preservation, as much as is possible, of our ways of life and our knowledge will include sending out ambassadors to as many places around the world as possible."

"And last but not least, we must prepare for the building of the labyrinth, exactly as the guides from the infinite have instructed. I feel confident that if we follow through on all of it, Atlantis will not vanish from the history of the world forever. "

CHAPTER 12
MIRA

The next morning at first light, Tia, Tenuen, Persephone and Integra assembled at Tenuen's private boat launch within the royal marina. It was a clear day, promising to be full of bright sunshine, and the breeze was constant but gentle—perfect conditions for pleasant sailing. The four smiled at one another in greeting, and as they clamored aboard Tenuen's boat, each silently wished that this could have been just another carefree excursion, and not the start of a serious, heartbreaking mission.

Ever since they had all learned to sail at the age of thirteen, the group had enjoyed many carefree trips with Tenuen at the helm and the others manning the sails and the boom. Most of their forays were on Tenuen's boat, since he was indisputably the one most enamored with sailing as well as the most proficient skipper among them. They never brought a crew aboard; Tenuen always captained his own craft. He loved being out at sea in the company of those closest to him.

Long ago, when they were still adventurous teens, the group had come across a small island less than a morning's sail northeast of the city of Atlantis. All of the youngsters fell in love right away with its rugged natural beauty, and enjoyed exploring the rocky terrain. They soon discovered that this island had a population of one. Mira was a round, sparkly, olive skinned, jovial woman. She was seemingly ageless, and the friends could never decide if she was as young as they were, or as old as time. What was certain is that she was wise. Mira had spent most of her early life on the mainland where she had attained the highest possible mastery in her studies of vibrational metaphysics, but had long since taken up residence on the small island, where she now inhabited a beautiful limestone cave.

As they settled into their places on the boat, Tenuen untied it from its moorings and took the helm. Persephone, functioning as first mate, waited for him to tell her to raise the sails. The sea was calm as the boat slipped almost silently from the marina and out into open water. Tia knew that if the wind picked up, she and Integra would be called upon to help, but for now they settled onto a bench in the stern of the boat. Tia gathered her long, loosely braided locks and fastened them against her head with a stick in an effort to stop the wind from batting them about. She tried to relax and direct her thoughts toward things that felt good. It was taking some focused concentration not to think about the real reason for this journey, and looking for a way to distract herself, Tia began observing her beloved from behind as he steered the boat. She thought she would never tire of looking at him, and that she was as deeply in love with him now as she had ever been. Integra noticed the trajectory of Tia's gaze and smiled, causing Tia to laugh a little with embarrassment. It was so good to have Tenuen back from his travels. If only now they could just joyfully plan their wedding. If only they didn't have to deal with the horrible ... no wait, there were those thoughts again... And again, she reined them in and cast about for things to appreciate.

Looking out at the sun rising in a rosy glow over the mountains, Tia felt her shoulders soften and fall, and she directed her mind to think about the friend they were on their way to see. Tia cherished her friendship with the always cheerful, endlessly interesting Mira. Of the four friends on the boat, Tia was the one who had spent the most time on the island, and Mira had imparted much to Tia over the course of their friendship. Smiling inwardly now at the thought of being once again in the presence of her dear and fascinating friend, Tia said aloud, "It will be so good to see Mira." Then she thought, "If only it wasn't for the reason..." Stop! It would be wonderful to see her, and to hear her singular ringing laugh. There, that felt better, and Tia, wanting to stay in that line of thinking, searched her memory for happier times and focused on those as they sailed along.

Tia, Integra, Persephone, and Tenuen had all studied the tenets of vibrational metaphysics and all of them had attained very high levels of achievement. However, Mira had surpassed them all in education and knowledge. She had received the highly respected title of Sage, something few Atlanteans attained. As a sage, she possessed the ultimate understanding of how the laws of vibrational metaphysics interact. She understood that the power that humans possess is based in their intentional use of energy and vibration. Mira's level of ability was such that she could actually manipulate both time and space. She knew that physical matter was really an illusion, because everything, including solid objects, is made up of vibrating energy. Mira was also known far and wide for having mastered the art of reading the stars, and Atlanteans of all walks of life and with all types of questions often made their way across the water to seek counsel on her little island.

After a few hours of smooth sailing, they pulled up to Mira's dock. As always, they were each struck anew by the sheer beauty of the place. Integra was the first to step onto the dock. "Looks like Mira's made her flower gardens even more magical! It seems this place becomes more wonderful every time we come!"

While it was true that Mira lived in a cave, it was not at all as one might expect. This cave was not dark, wet, or forbidding. Formed naturally in a large deposit of limestone, the cave had several window openings carved into the wall near the entrance, at staggered heights. Clear faceted crystals had been placed in all of these openings to refract and amplify the daylight and bring brightness into the home. The limestone on the island contained much iron, which gave it a pinkish hue. As the group entered the walkway that led to the main entry to the cave, they passed through an arched gate that Tia had fashioned herself. It was in fact one of the metal working projects she was most proud of. The gate was a sculpture depicting ocean waves and a seagull flying past the sun—as if reflecting the actual scene that was now behind them as they walked. Tia reached out and touched it as they passed into the courtyard.

As she always did when arriving at Mira's place, Tia felt a tingle of happy excitement and anticipation. The group followed the path leading to Mira's door. It was flanked on both sides by walls of the pale pink limestone, and along those walls Mira's gardens were a riot of color, bursting with flowers, plants and bushes that spilled over onto the walkway. There were interesting things everywhere one looked. Mira had made ornaments from odd bits of wood and hung them along the garden wall, and there were long purple spikes of lavender that she had harvested from the other side of the island and hung here to dry. In addition to the gates and doors, Mira had commissioned Tia to make smaller items, such as the sixcylinder chimes that hung above her front door and were now tinkling in the wind as the friends approached. Tia felt honored that her own art contributed to this gorgeous, high-energy setting. She felt her vibration rising to match the vibration of love and beauty that filled the air along this path.

At the very moment that the group reached her door, Mira swung it open wide, and her belly laugh rang out through the courtyard like a song. "Ha ha ha! So great of you to finally show up! You're just a little late!" Tia and Integra glanced at each other and smiled, as if to say to one another,

"Everything happens in perfect timing, and Mira knows this, yet she always makes that silly remark about us being being a little late!" "So good to see you all! Come in, come in! Ha ha HA!" Mira wrapped each of the friends in turn into a big bear hug, as they crossed the threshold and entered her living space. Her eyes sparkled. She loved having company, and while they often came to see her individually or in smaller groups, having all four of them together was a rare pleasure, left over from the times when all of them were younger and less constrained by their various duties.

The inside of the cave was a cozy and inviting retreat. Pale beige woven mats covered the floors, and the inner walls were covered in the same lovely white stone that was used to build most of the structures in Atlantis. In fact, it was every bit as light in the main living space within the cave as it was outside in the garden.

Tia drank in the sight of her lifelong friend and teacher. When Mira laughed, as she was doing now, her deep green eyes lit up and danced. They reflected the bright vibrant colors of the flowing robes she wore. Tia always delighted in seeing what new and interesting garment Mira was wearing, since her style was so different than what was common for the women of Atlantis. Even priestesses like Tia, Integra, and Persephone wore garments that while made of fine fabric, were usually monochrome and of a rather plain and utilitarian style. Mira's clothing was different. She often received gifts of multicolored and intricately patterned fabric from far away, brought by people who traveled from all ends of the planet to seek insights and answers from the stargazer about their life situations.

"Welcome, all of you!" Mira said again. "We will all have tea in just a moment, yes?" All four enthusiastically nodded their agreement. "Who would say no to your enchanted tea?" asked Tia.

The friends all took comfortable seats at a table in the lounge area near the main entrance to the cave and Mira disappeared into her adjacent kitchen. Everything was already laid out. Mira had somehow known to expect four visitors. Mira returned with a decanter of steaming, fragrant liquid, which she set on the table. Taking her place at the fifth place at the table, she began to pour out the tea. Each cup that she handed to one of her guests had a different color and scent. Tia's was a deep blood red, Tenuen's was golden brown, and Persephone and Integra received cups of pale yellow tea. All were delighted, and exclaimed that the tea was delicious and fragrant like no other. Tia had always wanted to know the recipe but when she'd asked in the past, Mira would just list some herbal ingredients, and perhaps honey, and nothing in what she said would explain the amazing ability of the tea to be different for each drinker! The friends had long ago accepted that there were magical things that happened when visiting Mira that would never be explained. Tia didn't feel the need to voice any questions or receive any explanations. She just enjoyed the moment and as everyone sipped the tea, the atmosphere in the cave was calm, yet full of expectation and anticipation, as the four friends knew they would soon be voicing what had brought them to this place today.

When everyone had consumed more than one cup of tea (Tia's second cup was yellow and Tenuen's second cup was blue), they left the table and arranged themselves on cushions on the floor. As they did so, the mood perceptibly became tenser, and Tenuen gestured to the women that he would address Mira first.

"Mira," he began, "We have come on this visit with a rather urgent need, so I will ask us to set aside any further socializing in order to get right to the business at hand."

Tenuen was in working mode, Tia noticed. His words and tone were now those of the King's Ambassador, rather than a lifelong acquaintance paying a friendly call. Tia knew he took this responsibility seriously, but she was a bit disappointed that they would not have more time to relax in Mira's company.

Mira stood up and bowed. "As always, I am ready to serve the

Kingdom and the royal family in whatever way I am able." Tenuen always appreciated when there was respect given, and he rose and bowed to his old friend in return. "Mira, we know of your powers of prophecy using the endless sky, so I wonder if you might have any inkling of why we have come here today?"

CHAPTER 13
MIRA DELIVERS HER TRUTH AND PROPHECY

Mira didn't answer right away. Then without speaking, she motioned for them all to get up and follow her through one of the doors that led to another area of the cave. None of the friends had ever been invited to go through that particular door and they had no idea what might lie within. The sculpted metal door was an exact replica of the one at the main entrance to Mira's dwelling. Tia knew that this door must lead to something special and interesting, but had never been so bold as to inquire about it.

Persephone and Tia looked at each other with raised eyebrows. They all followed Mira, and when she opened the door, they peered inside. The room was completely dark, and strangely no light seemed to spill in from through the open door. Everyone filed in, and Mira quickly shut the door behind them. Enveloped in inky darkness, they felt, although they could not see, a large expanse of open space around them. They stood silently waiting for whatever was to come next.

For a moment nothing seemed to be happening. Tenuen started to ask, "Mira, I don't think…" and in that very moment, suddenly a vision of a night sky appeared above and around them.

By the light of the stars and moon in this vision or illusion, they could see one another, and they saw that they were standing in a very large, empty room. On the walls, another vision was shown to them—their familiar city of Atlantis, spread out below a vast twinkling sky.

"My friends," Mira began to explain, "The sky, with all of its constellations, moons, and stars, reflects what is happening in our lives. Often this is misunderstood, and many believe that the stars and the planets directly affect us. It is believed that events in our lives can be caused by the movement or locations of celestial formations. However, this is a misconception. In truth, the sky is a mirror. It does not cause the events of our lives; it shows them to us. The sky is always *reflecting* the collective experience of humans. As a master Stargazer, when I speak of the future, I am describing what I see when the sky shows me visions of what is to come, based on what we humans have already created and how we are vibrating. Sometimes the future I see reflected can be changed—by changing our thoughts and behaviors—but sometimes, the momentum of what has been created by the masses is too great to stop, and the outcomes are inevitable. What you are about to see is an instance of the latter."

The prince and the three priestesses remained quiet as they gazed at the scene that twinkled and shone above and around them. Mira continued. "What you are looking at right now is the sky as it appeared exactly 25 moons ago."

"Notice those larger lights," said Mira, pointing. "See how they travel across the sky in the distance, considerably out of the way of Gaia's journeys around the sun?" The friends all nodded.

Mira waved her hand, and the vision above them changed. The lights that Mira had pointed out appeared much larger and closer. They now occupied a position between the moon and their planet, Gaia. "Mira," Tenuen's voice sounded smaller in the seeming vastness of the place they stood. "Is this what is happening now? What exactly are those lights that are approaching us?"

Mira sighed heavily. "I have no choice. One of my last jobs in this lifetime is to give all of you the answer to that question."

With another wave of Mira's hand, the two lights began to move across the sky. They changed direction and now seemed to be coming even closer and getting larger as they approached the vision of the city of Atlantis. The lights were both frightening and beautiful, trailed by long brilliant tails that were entrancing to behold. And then, as they all watched, in the vision one of the lights slammed into Gaia, and a huge explosion caused them all to jump and take a step back. There was immediately another terrifying crash as they watched the second great light collide with Gaia, directly hitting Atlantis.

The vision then disappeared in an instant. Again they were engulfed in complete darkness. Mira opened the door and beckoned them back to the brightly lit living area of the cave. They filed out, blinking against the sunlight that streamed in through the crystals in the walls, struggling to incorporate what they had just seen.

Without being asked or told, they walked to the table and took their original seats. Mira again filled their teacups from the decanter they had emptied before. It was somehow full again with steaming hot liquid, and this time they all received tea that appeared as a full spectrum rainbow color as it was poured, but turned to a murky brown once in their cups. Mira looked each of them in the eye in turn, and then said, "During this lifetime nothing has brought me greater joy than being able to be the harbinger of good news for my fellow humans, and to counsel those who come to me in ways to make their futures better. Alas, this time, I have no choice but to tell you a painful truth. I cannot let you go through the next six moons not knowing."

"Not knowing what?" Tia asked as they all leaned forward, giving Mira their full attention.

"Those lights you saw are comets. They are now on their way toward us. The explosions you saw are what will happen when they connect with the land of Atlantis." Mira went on. "I do not claim to understand it. In fact, I have never in all my time studying and exploring the stars come across anything like it. From my habitual watching of the night sky, I have for a long time known of the existence of these comets. Nothing ever indicated the likelihood of their collision with Gaia, let alone of directly hitting the exact location of our beloved Atlantis. So when I saw that the comets had changed their direction, I was surprised, and I could only surmise that vibrationally, things had changed in our world in such a way that the trajectory of the comets changed as well. Of course, I always operate under the general assumption that all is well, so perhaps I had not been paying close enough attention..." Mira seemed to forget the presence of the others and her face became drawn as she sank into thoughts of what appeared to be self-recrimination. "If only," she stammered in a quiet voice. "If only I had seen it sooner, maybe I could have helped to avert ... "

Never before had Tia seen her friend and mentor struggle with self doubt. Tia knew from her own experience the dark path this kind of thought could lead one down, and so she stood and walked over to her dear friend and gently placed her hand on Mira's arm.

Tia whispered softly, "Mira, you have done nothing amiss. As you said, this is all a result of the collective vibration. You have fulfilled your function with love and skill. You are a blessing to us, and we will use what you have told us for good. We already knew before we came here today that a darkness has been spreading in our communities, and it has gathered enough momentum that it now prevails. The darkness caused by humans trying to exert power and to dominate others has spread like a disease. We are approaching the end of our cycle and no one person's influence can stop the inevitable. The choice we have now is in how we respond to these conditions."

Tia knew that her friend's powerful mind was at work reorienting her thoughts, and soon Mira picked up her head and said, "Yes. Because the stars *reflect* humankind's experience, the shift in the comets happened as the darkness spread. So the darkness wins..."

Hearing that sentence, all four of the friends' heads shot up in surprise.

Persephone jumped from her chair and strode to the head of the table. She stood tall and spoke in a deep and methodical voice, as she had the day before when she channeled information from her inner being. "NO!" she almost shouted. "Not True! Never forget that the light always prevails. The darkness that now spreads through our society will never win. It serves a purpose. It is cleansing our civilization and allowing us an opportunity to be sure that what is good in it will spread to all corners of Gaia, where it can grow and thrive. Yes, the human experience has some rebalancing to do. But this does not mean the darkness wins. Atlantis will rise again! And when it does, it will be with a renewed strength and clarity."

Persephone came out of her trance and realized she was standing up. She looked around and went back to her chair and asked for a refill of rainbow tea. Integra said, "Thank you for that, Persephone. The truths you just channeled are known to all of us, but this was the perfect time for us to be reminded."

Persephone's words gave Mira the boost she needed to rally, and she now looked and sounded like her strong and capable self again. "Once I realized what was happening, and that it looked inevitable, I began calling you telepathically. I knew you would all come as soon as you could. I was not aware that you were receiving warnings of your own from other sources. We have exactly six moons to prepare. We must try to help as many Atlanteans as possible remove themselves from harm's way."

Mira's words were met by silence. Tia picked up her teacup, sensing that whatever was in it was good for her and knowing that she needed to ingest something good for her, right now. She downed its contents in one gulp. Her cup clattered to its saucer and she let out a loud uncontainable sob, laying her head on the table with a thud. Until now she had been strong. She had used all she knew about directing and aligning her emotions and had even been able to comfort Mira, But now, it suddenly sank in that only six moons from the present, life as they knew it would cease, and she found it almost impossible not to focus on just one fact: her beloved homeland would disappear. Gone would be the sacred buildings. The pyramids, the statues, the works of art, all would be gone. Her composure was even more shaken when her thoughts turned to the beasts of Atlantis, wild and domesticated alike. Picturing the demise of all the innocent creatures finally forced open the floodgates of Tia's tears.

Tenuen went wordlessly to Tia's side and put his arm around her, and Mira reached out to take her hand and hold it tightly. Tia kept weeping, as if she was shedding the collective tears of the group, and indeed for the entire civilization of Atlantis. She didn't even bother to try to stop herself from envisioning everything she loved being engulfed by water and lost forever. She turned toward Tenuen and collapsed into his embrace as she cried, until slowly her sobs subsided and she could breathe again.

Regaining her composure, Tia wiped her eyes on the cloth Mira proffered, and she started slowly to redirect her thoughts. As she did so, she felt herself rise up out of that deep, dark hole of fear she had fallen into. She closed her eyes and told herself silently, "I can purposefully choose thoughts that systematically take me up the scale of emotions. Every problem, no matter how intense and frightening, comes with its own solutions. Next steps to take will appear and our path will light up, when we allow ourselves to rise to meet it."

The others seemed to be silently grappling in a similar manner. They all knew they could not vibrate in resonance with the tragedy if they were to be a match to the hopeful actions they needed to take next.

Once Tia found herself in a stable enough vibration to speak, she told her friends that she had made the decision to focus on helping the citizens of Atlantis go somewhere new. "We Atlanteans must find a new land where we can bring forth future generations."

All at once Tia, Tenuen, Persephone, and Integra rose from the table, as if some unseen message had been delivered telling them it was time to leave. Mira rose as well, saying "I don't want to push you out the door, however, I know you have much to do, and want to get back on the boat while the sun it still high. You all have a heavy responsibility now that you know. The future of Atlantis depends on you. I cannot selfishly keep you near me..."

Tia exclaimed, "But Mira, I will be back; I must be back, I must see you again." She felt the tears well up in her eyes again at the thought that this could be goodbye. "I will be back soon, I will, and we will have a lovely day, as usual." Mira looked deeply into Tia's eyes and willed her to be stable, at least long enough to get them through their farewells. "Yes, yes, of course we will!" she confirmed, and everyone knew the lightness in her voice was forced.

Mira planted a kiss in the center of each guest's forehead, and they climbed back onto the boat, ready to head home. Tenuen did not jump right to the wheel, as he usually did. He could feel that the women were perhaps pondering a destination for them other than back to the royal marina. He voiced the suggestion that they go somewhere to rejuvenate first, and the others quickly agreed. "What about the sacred fern pools?"

The pools were located not far from where they were docked, on an even smaller island than Mira's. It was a place they often went to find spiritual renewal. Tia looked at Tenuen, and something in his expression made her quickly agree. Persephone and Integra also nodded, almost with relief. They knew they needed to go somewhere to gain calm and clarity before returning to the main island.

CHAPTER 14
MAIDENHAIR FALLS

Tenuen made sure everyone was safely aboard, Integra and Persephone readied the sails, and Tia cast off the lines, each of them moving as if by rote, while their minds were elsewhere. How does one deal with knowing that, along with a handful of friends, you must guide your entire civilization through the period leading to its imminent demise? Never before had their ability to take things moment by moment been so tested. They knew they had to purposefully align their thoughts to the best possible outcome, and purposefully align they did, while the familiar tasks associated with getting Tenuen's boat out of harbor and out to sea kept their hands and bodies busy.

After a short sail, a small jut of land came into sight, sticking out of the water like a finger rising from the depths and pointing to the heavens. In no time they were again on dry land, hiking along the short path to a waterfall they had long ago dubbed Maidenhair Falls, after the rare maidenhair ferns that grew in lush abundance all around this small island. The tiny oasis was an exquisite and magical place, and the waterfall that spanned ten times the height of a man was its most alluring feature.

The path took them past palm trees that swayed in the gentle breeze, making a soothing rustling sound that allowed Tia to relax. She felt her shoulders release their tension, even as she realized this would likely be the last time she would visit this sacred spot. She stopped momentarily and stood listening to the wind, her eyes closed, willing herself to banish that thought. Then, quickening her step to catch up with the others, she moved quickly to Tenuen's side, and he put his arm around her as they walked toward the falls where they had spent so many happy times together as a couple.

As they approached, the sound of the rushing water grew louder, and though Tia continued to struggle with sad and fearful thoughts, as she shifted her attention to her breathing, and to their rhythmic footfalls on the path, she felt her vibration rising, so that when they came into the clearing and the falls were in sight, the powerful rush of the water washed away all thoughts. She broke into a run toward the pool of water surrounding the bottom of the falls. She disrobed quickly and dove in with a joyful whoop.

The moment she felt the water engulf her, she was tapped into the joy of previous visits, and felt nothing but happiness and wholeness. The others followed suit and in moments they were all splashing in the fresh and invigorating waters.

Persephone had always loved to swim over to the waterfall and stand in the calm water behind it. She did that now, and watching the powerful cascade, she thought about how the violence of the water falling so close to her peaceful refuge was a metaphor for all that was taking place in their lives.

Time seemed to stand still as each of the friends did their best to take in all the joy and peace this last visit to the falls could offer. When the sun had just begun to go behind the trees, they ceased their joyful carousing and gathered at the furthest spot from the crashing water, where sitting on rocks in the shallowest part of the pool, they commenced a somber meeting, ready to discuss their next moves.

Tenuen began. "Of course, I will immediately inform my

father." The others nodded and murmured in agreement. Tenuen, who always sat with a straight back and spoke forthrightly, was now hunched forward, his chin tucked to his chest, as if the thought of being the bearer of such tidings to the king was more than he could stand. Then he breathed deeply and straightened, intentionally pulling his shoulders back, and looking directly into the eyes of each of his dear friends one by one, he asked, "Please, will you all come with me?"

The three priestesses were taken aback at the sight of Tenuen being vulnerable and needing support, but not one of them raised an eyebrow, and in unison they spoke their agreement. "Of course. We will be honored." With that, Tenuen relaxed a bit and flashed a boyish grin that was so engaging that all three women smiled back, despite the gravity of the situation. "It's settled then. We will go together and present Father with the horrible news, and discuss with him what we've formulated as a plan to deal with it."

Well before the sun had descended all the way into the ocean, the friends had quite easily arrived at a general plan. They all agreed that after bringing the news to the king, they would inform the Atlantean population of what was to occur. Then, they would take action to relocate as many souls as possible to safe havens in other lands.

In addition to saving people, the friends knew they had been entrusted with preserving and disseminating all of the information, knowledge, and wisdom of Atlantis. By using the powers inherent in crystals, and by building the labyrinth according to Persephone's vision, they would be able to gift all humans who would come after them with the essence of Atlantis. This, they knew, was no less a sacred and important a task than that of saving the lives of those who were in the path of destruction.

Tia was the first to jump out of the water. Holding out her hand, she gave each of her friends a boost onto dry land, and soon they were dressed and headed back to the boat. Nobody spoke along the trail or on the sail home, and the trip seemed to pass quickly, perhaps too quickly. It was the last trip of its kind for this group of four fast friends, in this particular lifetime.

When they disembarked at the Atlantis marina, none of them wanted to waste time getting ready for their meeting with King Aztlan. This was not to be a normal audience with the king, after all. They were going to see him without being summoned or giving prior notice of their arrival. And as Tenuen reminded them, "Aztlan may be the king, but he is also my father, and he is used to entertaining people in all states of dishevelment. Our mission is urgent. Let's go straight to see him."

CHAPTER 15
MEETING WITH THE KING

Twilight was now descending upon the city, and Tenuen knew his father would have retired to his pipe and books by now, so they all walked quickly to the pyramid building, and once inside, the women followed Tenuen to Aztlan's study. The king's attendant was just exiting the private chamber, quietly closing the door behind him, when he came face to face with Tenuen and the three priestesses. If he was surprised at how they were all a bit out of breath and looked like they'd just hurried in without giving a thought to their appearance, he didn't show it. He smiled at them and gave an easy small bow. "I shall have more refreshments delivered immediately. Is there anything you require or prefer?" He addressed Tenuen, but included all four of them in his glance. Tenuen thanked the man and asked him to bring whatever food and drink was available and easily prepared.

The attendant nodded, and left them.

Tenuen raised his hand to knock, and at the very same moment, Aztlan threw open the study door, and beamed his delight as he welcomed them all, exclaiming, "Ah!" as they filed into the cozy room. The king pulled the entire group to his expansive chest in a warm hug.

King Aztlan stood head and shoulders above them all, Tenuen included. He was a robust man whose bright green eyes were usually smiling, and the curly yellow hair that grew past his shoulders, bounced when he laughed. His white and gold robes smelled of chamomile and lavender, essential oil scents that were prevalent throughout the interior of the pyramid. Tia always felt safe and loved in the presence of this man who had felt more like a friend than a ruler. She could not recall a single time she had not left a meeting with him feeling uplifted for having been in his presence. Often she had noted that surely this was what made him such great leader. He didn't lead so much as he allowed. He allowed the people to come and express themselves, and he helped them find ways to make their desires come to fruition. By doing this he was able to preside over a kingdom of happy and fulfilled citizens who were valued for who and what they were. The donkey and the dolphin were as revered in Aztlan's eyes as the human or the demi-god. His heightened ability to read and understand people and situations and to see all sides of issues made him a remarkable statesman, able to find the common ground among those who disagreed, sometimes on very divisive issues.

All this flashed through Tia's thoughts as she looked around Aztlan's study. Similar to Tenuen's private quarters, it had mats on the floor that were cool and comforting to walk on, and an ample collection of upholstered settees and carved wooden chairs with plump cushions. The walls displayed intricate tapestries of realistic scenes from around Atlantis. They depicted blooming orchards, barnyards full of magnificent livestock, and majestic ships floating in the various ports throughout the kingdom. A large map also hung on the wall, the legend showing the distribution of the population. Most of the four million inhabitants of the kingdom lived on the islands and in the ocean front port cities along the coasts of three of Gaia's largest landmasses. One million citizens were residents of the capital city of Atlantis.

Tenuen, Tia, Persephone, and Integra normally would have

been tired, yet exhilarated, after a day of sailing, visiting Mira, and hiking to Maidenhead Falls. Today, however, when they sat back into the comfortable seating surrounding Aztlan's chair, they were all simply exhausted. They tried to hide it from the king, since they knew custom dictated they not reveal the reason for their visit until after partaking in some food and drink. And anyway, they were ravenous. Having consumed nothing since early that morning except for Mira's special tea, the four gratefully accepted the offerings brought promptly by Aztlan's attendant. The king watched and continued to beam as his guests enjoyed fresh meat and crab and warmed spiced fruit. Each also accepted a glass of wine.

When Tenuen had assuaged the most urgent part of his appetite, he realized he'd been eating very quickly, and slowed down enough to pay some attention to his father. He felt a pang when he saw how pleased his father was to have them there. Little did he know, Tenuen thought, that the occasion for their visit was the bearing of shocking news. And while he knew his father would never blame the message on the messenger, he deeply wished he didn't have to be the one to bring him the devastating information.

As the meal drew to its inevitable end, Tenuen thought, "I've always been able to act decisively and take control of a situation, so I may as well start doing that now." He drained the last of his wine, wiped his mouth, and stood up. The three priestesses and King Aztlan all looked up at him expectantly.

"Father," Tenuen began, his voice faltering, exactly as he had hoped it wouldn't. Aztlan allowed his son to collect himself, but when Tenuen attempted to go on, the king raised the palm of his hand as if to say, "stop". His deep voice was soothing yet forceful, "You may be still, my son. Please sit back down and hear me now. I have learned all about what has transpired for you recently. I know you have been gathering information to present to me. You have exhibited great integrity in circumstances that may easily have caused you to falter. I am aware of all of it, and I respect the actions you have taken. I take pride in the way you have conducted yourself."

Of course! Tia's thoughts swam. Of course Aztlan had no need to hear the story from their lips; he had his own ways of getting information and news! He must have sensed that Tenuen had undergone something profound during his travels, and that he had returned bearing a burden he was reluctant to share. Tia thought it had been silly of them to even entertain the thought that they needed to inform him. But, she wondered, how exactly did he come into possession of the information? Persephone had not arranged an audience with him for Tarkus, and she had not told him of her visions, and Tenuen had not yet briefed him about his trip! Could Mira have shared her prophetic visions with the king? Breaking into Tia's musings, Aztlan began to explain.

Smiling softly and sadly at his youngest son, he said "I have been king for a long time, and I have many sources of intelligence, as you know. Some of my messengers are winged, and some four-legged, but for this, I consulted the most powerful source that I have at my behest—The Orichalcum Bowl of Sight. There were inklings of things, very upsetting and disappointing things happening in the lands of my two eldest sons. It was because I was so loath to believe these things that I sent you, Tenuen, my youngest son and most trusted intelligence gatherer, on your mission. As hard as it was to fathom that my own sons could have been gathered into the darkness, I knew I needed to learn the truth." As the king spoke this last, his face took on a haggard expression, and Tenuen thought he had never seen his father look so sad, or so old.

"When you returned, Tenuen, seeming out of sorts and needing some time to gather yourself before making your report, I wondered if you had seen things that you knew would not be easy for me to be told. Then today, when I was informed that the four of you had shipped out at dawn toward Mira's island, I knew it was time to employ the Bowl of Sight, and to see for myself what was afoot."

Tia, Persephone and Integra sat mouths agape. They had never even heard of the Orichalcum Bowl of Sight. They were utterly fascinated at this latest revelation of King Aztlan's abilities. Tenuen had heard of the Bowl, and knew it could be used by the king for scrying, but had never seen it or been told anything directly about Aztlan's experiences with it. Tia thought about the wonders she'd had no knowledge of before today. She thought about Mira's ability to conjure the sky in her special room, and now Aztlan's ability to see past, present and future in his Bowl of Sight. She wondered what other hidden magical things she might discover. All four friends sat forward and listened intently as Aztlan continued.

The king recounted for them what he had seen in the Orichalcum Bowl of Sight, and they all recognized the details from Tarkus's accounts of his scrying, from Persephone's visions and channeling, from Tenuen's first hand experiences, and from Mira's revelations. Aztlan knew everything. They were glad it was not their first hearing of all of this, so that they were able to accept it with some stability. Tenuen was especially relieved, since he was not, after all, the one delivering the news to his father.

CHAPTER 16
A GLIMPSE OF THE FUTURE

King Aztlan smiled, sat up straight in his chair, breathed deeply, and said, "As always, it is wise for us to focus our attention forward rather than backward. And with that in mind, dear ones, you are all going to have a new experience. You see, I have yet another powerful way to seek guidance and insight: The traveling room. It is as yet unknown to any of you. Had you been able to continue your studies, you would each have been initiated into its workings when you had passed your sage level trainings. We now know that is never to happen, so I have decided to reveal the room to all four of you today, and together we will consult it regarding the profound events that we have so recently been given knowledge of."

The four sat and drank in his words. None of them could think of any response, though their thoughts were spinning. They had no idea such a thing even existed, much less what it might be able to provide or what it had offered the king all this time. But the king was still speaking and they turned their attention back to him.

"Always when there have been questions of greatest import to the kingdom, I have gone to the traveling room and journeyed by myself, I have always kept my travels private. This time, though, will be different. Each of you has already responded to the news of what is imminent for our kingdom in ways that have made me proud. You have met the situation at hand, and you will be the ones to shepherd our kingdom through its next phase. The traveling room will be a powerful tool to help you in that endeavor. Our journey will provide a meaningful contribution to your knowledge and understanding, and will inform your next steps.

The king beamed at them, and they beamed back at hearing that they were to be introduced to a new aspect of the most powerful inner workings of the kingdom. They were all intensely curious now as to what this traveling room would entail.

Integra put her hand to her forehead as she felt a tingling run across her skull. She knew this meant that something powerful was happening and that she was in accord with her highest spiritual self. Persephone felt something too—a lightness of being, uplifting her with excitement about what could possibly be coming next. Tia and Tenuen reached for one another's hands as they leaned forward to take in what Aztlan was about to reveal.

The king stood up and said he would leave them briefly, and requested that they retire to the guest quarters to bathe and don fresh robes. After that they were to reconvene at the door to the king's study.

When they gathered again at the entrance to Aztlan's chambers, they became momentarily disoriented. Next to the door they had entered before, there was another door that none of them had been aware of earlier. Tenuen looked around, confused. He had been in and out of his father's chambers thousands of times over the course of his life, and it was very puzzling that a new door should suddenly appear.

Aztlan greeted them and moved quickly to stand in front of the unfamiliar door. His imposing figure was now dressed in white and gold robes, and he carried a white and gold scepter topped with a brilliant crystal at the top. Turning toward the new door, Aztlan lifted his scepter and brought it down firmly to the floor, tapping three times. At that, the door swung open to reveal a dark and narrow hallway angled steeply upward, with no windows or apparent openings. Ducking his head, the king entered first and beckoned the others to follow. When they were all inside, Aztlan handed Tenuen the scepter, and using both of his hands, he closed the door firmly behind them. As he did so, the door vanished and become part of the seamless stone wall of the passageway. Repossessing his scepter, the king then took the lead, and the group climbed swiftly through the darkness. The crystal on Aztlan's scepter faintly shimmered in the darkness and provided the only light as they made their way up the passageway.

The four friends had to hurry to keep up with the king. Tenuen smiled at the sight of his father veritably scampering, something he could not recall ever having seen before.

After continuing upward in this manner for what felt to the four friends like a long time, Aztlan took an abrupt left turn, and stopped abruptly. Tenuen was close behind his father, and saw they were standing in front of another door. This one was made of heavy metal and looked like the door to a large vault. After lifting the long metal lever that fell across the front of this door, Aztlan leaned his scepter against the wall of the passageway, put his palms against the door and said, "Open please."

The door swung open, and as Tenuen got a glimpse of what was inside he could not hold back and let out a small cry of surprise. All three women were just then coming quickly around the turn, and they piled in behind him in a jumble. Integra was the first to enter, and she stopped in her tracks so quickly that Persephone ran right into her, and when Tia careened around the corner she hit the whole group with a thud!

Aztlan, having scooted through the doorway first, had stepped quickly to the side and let the pile-up happen. Seeing him smile with mirth at them all bumping into one another, Tenuen wondered for a moment if his father, ever the jester, had actually planned it that way.

Once everyone was standing upright again, they took in their surroundings. They had clearly arrived at the very top of the pyramid building. The ceiling of the very large room came to a point in the center, high above their heads. Openings in the walls and ceiling housed large crystals that brought the moonbeams tumbling in, causing magical patters of light to dance all over every surface. The full moon was bright, and the crystals afforded them clear vision.

The momentary silliness subsided, and the four friends walked slowly and reverently about the room, taking in all the details. The walls, floor, and ceiling were made of large sheets of pink quartz crystal with veins of orichalcum running through them forming lines and striations that looked like drawings. Tia and Integra were completely enthralled. This looked so similar to the material they had used in the fashioning of their healing pod, which just yesterday they had declared ready for use. They had thought that they were the first to use this powerful mix, but here it was on a much grander scale, in this magnificent room that had obviously been here for quite some time.

In the center of the room stood a large square partitioned area. This too was made of stone covered with orichalcum and pink crystal. It contained six long reclining chairs made of the same material. These chairs were situated in the middle of the box, such that the feet of those lying on them would come into contact with the orichalcum and crystal on the walls of the partition.

Integra moved closer to one of the outer walls of the room and gingerly reached out to touch it. Aztlan smiled his encouragement of her exploration, and Tia also looked closely, sharing a look with Integra that was full of meaning. Tia and Integra were flooded simultaneously with understanding that this orichalcum and crystal mix was indeed as powerful as they had thought. And they knew now that they had not discovered it so much as they had attuned themselves to it. They had tapped into a knowing that had allowed them to use this ancient, perhaps even eternal, formula.

There was little talking as the friends took in this new spectacle. The walls were constructed in such a way that what appeared to be a solid crystal covering was actually a many-layered textured material. In some places it looked much like a map, with outlines and borders of continents and kingdoms and planetary systems laid out in orichalcum. As they looked at the walls, pictures emerged. As they moved about the room and changed their perspective, or when the light changed, the pictures changed. These pictures were intricate, detailed, shimmering visions.

Integra pointed at one of the walls saying, "I see the Orion star system. And the Pleiades. And over here I see our beloved planet and the entire celestial arena surrounding it." "That is correct," Aztlan beamed.

Aztlan allowed them to explore the room and take everything in, while he continued to give them information about it. "This was all done by the ancient priests who perfected this craft even before the Kingdom of Atlantis existed. They developed this process to show our entire universe, with each separate element discernable within the complete whole." Again, Tia and Integra were overwhelmed with the knowing that they had tapped into what the masters had created so long ago. The crystals and the orichalcum were used here to create an entire room of stunning art.

"Now", said Aztlan, "I will explain why I brought you to this upper chamber. The traveling room is a portal from which to enter into out of body travel for the purpose of asking questions and receiving answers from the Universe. We rendezvous with exactly the answers we need, even when we may not be sure of what to ask. Through this portal we are led to the information that is for our highest good. The vibrations of this room will guide us into the field, where we will be given the most important information for us, individually and collectively. For this journey, we will stay together as a group. I have faith that what we will be shown today will help us all to feel better about what is coming."

The mention of the need to feel better brought everyone back to the real questions at hand. They had been so enthralled with what they found in Aztlan's upper chamber that they had momentarily forgotten the somber news they were all dealing with that was the reason they were going on this journey!

Aztlan's voice was soothing and calm. "Let us embark then, on a journey together to seek more information about what is coming for Atlantis. We will meet again in the field." With that, the king moved into the partitioned enclosure, removed his shoes, and selected a chair to recline on. It immediately seemed to become much longer than the others and it accommodated his huge frame. The others quickly followed suit, and once everyone had taken off their shoes and lay back in the chairs, they placed the soles of their feet in direct contact with the crystals and orichalcum of enclosure walls.

Tenuen had been holding his father's scepter, and as he laid it beside his chair the light from the scepter's crystal that had lit their way up the hidden passage was extinguished. The room was alive with shimmering moonbeams that danced all around them.

The scenes on the walls and ceiling continuously shifted and changed. One moment they showed a representation of the celestial theatre, and then suddenly there were maps of the countries and continents of Gaia. Then those maps were overlaid with the intricate energy lines that ran through the planet.

It had been a long, tumultuous day, exhausting both physically and emotionally. As excited and profoundly curious as they all were, they wondered if they would be able to stay awake for this new experience. That worry was fleeting, however, since almost immediately upon settling into their seats the subtle vibrations emanating from crystals and orichalcum that made up the traveling apparatus had an invigorating effect on them all.

Tia's eyes adjusted to the moonlight and she was completely

enthralled with what was happening on the walls. She wanted to see more of this light show, but she soon felt her eyelids grow heavy. She noticed that her friends' breathing had become heavier and more even, and she gave herself over to the familiar experience of leaving her body and going out to the field. Closing her eyes, she did not sleep, but felt her body release its connection to the physical structure she sat on, and then the gentle release of the essence of her spirit as well, and she floated freely.

In what seemed like just a split second, she was with her friends again. The three priestesses, the prince, and the king were all sitting together in the fancy box seats at a gilded theater, waiting for the curtain to open and a play to begin. They were the only spectators in the audience for this play. Tia looked around, thinking that in all of her experiences in the field, she had never been shown a play on a stage. She settled back into the velvet seat and felt deep relaxation come over her, just as if she had brought her physical body with her, and although she knew of course the she had not, she marveled at how the field allowed her to feel such relief and release. Glancing around at her comrades she saw that they too seemed to be in a state of calm anticipation.

Suddenly spotlights illuminated the curtain and it parted to reveal the stage. The group looked down from their high seats, and leaned forward as a scene took shape before them. The stage was set with a configuration of stones and lush coiffed bushes. The stones and bushes formed what looked like a piece of a maze. Recognition hit Tia and Persephone at once and they exclaimed, "A labyrinth!" They only saw a piece of a labyrinth, but knowing flowed through them as they recognized their future creation.

As if acknowledging their awareness and responding to it, the scene then expanded before their eyes. The stage moved toward them and now they could see a larger portion of the labyrinth. When the stage stopped they could discern an actor. It was a man, sitting cross-legged on a large purple amethyst crystal. The man had a short white beard and long white hair tied with a leather string. Even with his white hair, he seemed ageless. The suit he wore—trousers, shirt, jacket, and tie—was pure white.

Another actor entered the scene. A lovely woman, ageless as well, walked along the path between the stones, engrossed in her thoughts as she moved, and not noticing the man. The large amethyst crystal was situated at a crossroads in the labyrinth, and when the woman looked up to decide which way to turn, the man shot his leg out and tripped her! She stumbled and fell right on top of him with an exclamation of surprise. She did not appear to be hurt, but it took her a moment to regain her composure after disentangling herself from the man and standing upright again. As she dusted herself off, he excitedly said, *"Well, Ping! Here you are finally! Do you have any idea how long I've been waiting here for you?"*

The woman looked at him, confused, and he rambled as if to himself, *"I've waited for a millennium, that's how long. Every day, right here, on this very spot..."* The man sighed, and looking at the woman with a bit of reprimand on his face, he asked, *"What on Earth have you been doing for the past millennium, Ping?"*

The woman peered into his sharp, clear eyes. Even from where the five Atlanteans sat those eyes looked bright blue. Then they flashed green, and then blue again, then one was blue and other green! The watchers noticed that the man's face looked extremely wrinkled now, but very kind.

"What in the world do you mean, where have I been for the last millennium? What kind of question is that?" said Ping.

"Oh Puh-leeze! Have you really forgotten?" the man seemed disgusted and disappointed at the thought.

At that moment a second woman entered from stage left, and walked up behind Ping in the labyrinth.

When the second woman's eyes became visible to the watchers, all five gasped with knowing recognition. "It's me," whispered Tia, her eyes glued in wonder to the woman on the stage. She was blond and beautiful, like Tia, but it was not her physical traits that brought about the recognition, it was her vibration. Each of the watchers recognized the very essence of Tia's soul radiating from the woman in the play. They watched with rapt attention as the second woman walked right up to the man, who was still sitting on his amethyst, and asked," *So, are you an angel? How do you know my friend Ping? I heard you tell her you've been waiting for her.*"

The man beamed with happiness, clapped his hands and almost bounced with glee. "*Sophie! So great to finally see you again*!" The two women on stage exchanged glances, eyebrows raised. It was clear to the watchers that neither of the female characters had a clue who the man might be, nor how he knew their names. They did not seem frightened, but they were mightily confused and curious.

The man responded, "*Oh no no no no. I'm not an angel. Not by any means or measure! Why would you ask that?*" Then, looking down at his garments, "*Oh, is it the suit? Is it because it's so whiiiiite?*" The man dragged out some of his words in an odd but endearing drawl. "*Anyway, no. Definitely not an angel*!" he laughed. "*I just like the suit. Mark Twain had one just like it, you know. I was one of his editors, in that lifetime. Crazy bastard. Acerbic wit. Stubborn as a she-goat. Raged when you changed a word...*"

"*Um,*" Ping interrupted his rambling, looking very confused. "*As interesting as that story is...who are you?*"

"*And how do you know our names*?" added Sophie.

"*Do you really remember nothing at all? Either of you*?" he seemed genuinely surprised, looking back and forth from one to the other, his hands and eyes upturned. Shaking his head, he sighed impatiently.

"*You called me here! So here I am! You, however, are just a little late!*"

With that the man uncrossed his legs, stood up, and joined them on the path of the labyrinth.

"*You can call me Murry.*"

"*Murry?*" repeated Sophie and Ping skeptically.

"*Yes. Murry. What? Were you expecting something long, Greek, and ancient? Well, I was Murry in one of my favorite incarnations. I was a wandering minstrel in Olde Britain. I wandered freely wherever I fancied, and got fed and housed for entertaining royalty. I was famous for my rhymes, you know.*"

"*Well, that's lovely, but it's got nothing to do with us.*" Sophie had already grown impatient to move on. Grabbing Ping's hand, she tried to pull her around the bend of the labyrinth, away from Murry.

Before they could get out of earshot, Murry spoke up in a louder and firmer voice than he'd used before, "*You have both suffered greatly. I'm truly so very sorry that it came to that. You are not crazy. No matter how others have been inclined to label you, you are not crazy. You have been seeing and hearing things all your lives, and have been told these were hallucinations. They were not. You are gifted. Gifted shamans. Both of you.*"

Sophie and Ping stopped short right after they heard "suffered greatly," and listened, still facing away from Murry.

The Atlantean time traveling watchers in the velvet seats were ever more fascinated.

"*Gifted,*" repeated Murry, "*Very gifted.*"

Sensing he had the women's attention now, even though their backs were still turned, some of the softness returned to Murry's tone. "*Ping, you are able to see things that look like they are three things, when others can see just one.*"

At that, Ping turned abruptly back toward Murry, wide-eyed. Murry continued. "*All your life, you have been able to see interdimensionally. Do you think everyone can do that? Well they can't. Nobody else has ever been able to do it. Well, except for the cats. But that's another story. I've been following you both since you were born into your present lifetime, and long before that. Some things called me away for a while, and when I came back you were both in a loony bin in America, convinced by the crazies there that you were the insane ones! Well, it's not true, and never has been."* Murry shook his head sorrowfully.

"I take responsibility," Murry sounded contrite. *"I should never have left off watching you. I believed that you would be able recollect your metaphysical training from previous lifetimes, and that you'd come to understand on your own what was happening to you in this one. But, you didn't. Oh well, never mind, we're here now, and we can begin again from where we are."*

As he spoke, Sophie and Ping retraced their steps back to where Murry stood. The Atlanteans sat still in the theater seats, waiting for the women's reaction to these revelations.

"So," Sophie slowly approached Murry again. *"You somehow know a lot about me and Ping. But what is really going on here?"*

"Well," Murry sighed, *"since you don't seem to remember a thing, I will have to fill you in. Let's sit down on these crystals over here and I'll give you all the info."*

The women sat, Sophie a bit more reluctantly than Ping, and Murry went on.

"Thirteen thousand years ago, the Kingdom of Atlantis was destroyed in what is now widely known as the Flood of Noah. The once high vibrating and illustrious Atlantean civilization had taken a turn toward the darkness, you see. Such a large number of its citizens had attuned themselves to a vibration that was not in resonance with the light or with their highest good, that the kingdom attracted its own downfall."

Turning to Sophie, he said, *"You were a Priestess of Atlantis in that lifetime. You and your closest friends knew of the coming destruction in advance. It was portended in the stars, and in other ways. You informed the Atlantean people of the comets that were on an unstoppable collision course toward Earth and of the flood that was on its way."*

When neither Sophie nor Ping made any response, Murry stood and began to pace in front of them as he spoke, again directing his remarks to Sophie.

"You and a small group of your closest comrades were given channeled instructions for the planning and the building of this very labyrinth in which we sit. This labyrinth holds all the accumulated knowledge of the thousands of years of Atlantean civilization."

Murry looked at Sophie, then at Ping, and seeming satisfied that they were going to remain stationery, he continued. *"As you know, we humans of the 21st century after Christ's birth are again experiencing a cycle of being out of sync with our highest good. The Atlanteans understood that the knowledge they had accumulated during their heyday could provide future humans the ability to bring it all back to the fore. They knew that Atlantis could rise again. And well, here we are, and it's for us, I mean you, to save the world again. So, are you ready to move through the labyrinth and learn what they knew and had accomplished in the mighty civilization that was Atlantis?"*

Sophie burst out in a loud guffaw. *"Okay, so, I'm the one who is supposed to be crazy, but this guy takes the cake."* She stood up as if to say she'd had enough of this circus, but Ping remained seated. Sophie sounded impatient now. *"C'mon Ping, let's go! This Murry guy just shows up and tells us that we are here to save the world, and he's saying it as if he's telling us what's for lunch. Like, no big deal. Can't you see he's at least one card short of a deck?"*

Ping smiled. *"Yeah, it does sound pretty far out there. But, there is something about this guy."* She spoke to Sophie as if Murry wasn't present, her voice softly imploring. *"He feels familiar to me somehow. Like maybe he's a long lost uncle or brother of mine, or someone I knew in a past life that I agreed to rendezvous with in this life. I feel we can trust him. There is something here. It feels like something real."*

Murry was grinning now, and clapping. *"Ah, so you do remember! At least it's a vibrational memory, and that's good enough for me!"* He opened his arms and Sophie watched as Ping stood up and walked forward to be enveloped in his hug. When they broke their embrace, a shimmery white glow was seen emanating from all around Ping.

In the theater seats, the three priestesses, the prince, and the king, all sighed audibly.

On the stage, Murry grinned. "Magic," he said, "Magic."

CHAPTER 17
"IT'S UP TO US"

Five pairs of eyes were still trained on the stage as a thick curtain fell over it, and the house lights in the theater went on. Just as Tia's non-physical self was starting to adjust to the abrupt disappearance of the labyrinth and the vision of her future, she found herself physically adjusting her position on the lounge in the traveling room. She opened her eyes. The moonbeams still danced around the room as if unconcerned with any human drama, and the walls still projected their sparkly images. Tia felt as if she was waking from a dream, yet she knew she had been wide awake and had experienced a profound glimpse into the future of her spirit. Her feet still touching the orichalcum of the traveling pod, she felt a knowing course through her. "I will be Sophie," she whispered to herself. "An interesting name. So far in the future. And I will walk the labyrinth we have yet to build in this life." Her next thought filled her with awe and reverence. "And what we will discover there will help turn future humanity back toward the light."

Tia looked again around the room, at its twinkling lights and changing scenes on the walls. She felt relaxed, whole, and at one with creation, yet at the same time energized and infused with purpose. As Tia sat up and put her shoes back on, she saw that Tenuen, Integra, and Persephone were doing the same. Nobody had yet spoken, but there was a feeling of increased energy passing among all the friends. Their trip to the quantum field by way of the traveling room had shown them so much! How brilliant the Universe was to show them the future in the form of a stage play!

As they all got up from the traveling chairs, the last to rise from repose was Aztlan. He moved slowly and silently, looking at no one, with head bowed, toward the door.

Tenuen quickly retrieved his father's scepter from where he had laid it before their travels, and the four friends scrambled to follow the king. They exited the upper chamber and retraced their steps down the narrow passageway. The friends needn't have hurried, because the descent was slow. Unlike earlier, when they had followed their agile, ageless king upwards through the pyramid, this time he was moving with the measured gait of a person who feels the effects of advanced age. The low ceiling of the passageway necessitated bending over for such a tall man, yet even when they arrived back at Aztlan's study, the king did not rise to his full stature, but remained stooped. Tenuen felt a pang of worry, and wondered how his father could seem to have aged so much in such a short time.

Aztlan sat down heavily, and the friends followed suit, making themselves comfortable in the same seats they had previously occupied. The king motioned something to his attendant who had slipped silently into the chamber, and the five sat in silence, each in his own way assimilating what they had been shown while on their journey, until presently they were served herbal tea. Tenuen spoke up first. "Father, we would be pleased to have your assessment of all we were shown on the journey and indeed all we now know about our situation."

Aztlan stood, his limbs unfolding woodenly, and walked to where his son sat. His eyes darkened, yet they also looked full of love, as he placed his hand on Tenuen's shoulder and spoke in a voice that sounded a little more like his usual self. "Son, we here in Atlantis have had a blessed existence. Our lives have been full and rich and we have achieved success in every area of human endeavor. We have experienced the best of everything available to humankind. Now, this cycle of thriving is coming to an end."

Tenuen lifted his eyes to his father's as if willing him to continue. "I am satisfied," continued the king. "I am satisfied because I know, especially after what we were shown in the traveling room, that what we Atlanteans have experienced, learned, and created will continue beyond us. We leave soon, to be sure, but we leave a well-preserved legacy for our future selves, and for all future generations of humans."

Aztlan sighed, and when he next spoke he sounded again like a muchaged version of the king they had known all their lives. He took his eyes away from his son and glanced at each of the women in turn. "I trust that you will all do your parts as you have been bidden. The journey from which we have just returned has illuminated and answered much. You did not, as it turned out, need my guidance during our travels, and you do not need my guidance now, as you usher our civilization through its demise. The visionplay we were shown told us how extremely important the creation of the initiation labyrinth is. I know you will take care of that, and all that needs to be tended to before Atlantis as we know it comes to an end. I trust you all. I'm proud of you all. I thank you for your integrity, your creativity, your intelligence, your love, and your conviction. And now, you must excuse me."

And with that, King Aztlan of Atlantis turned toward the inner door to his bedchamber. The attendant sprang to aid and escort the tired king, and the prince and three priestesses remained sitting, as if in shock.

Tenuen stared at the door that had just swallowed his father, and his heart broke with the realization that this had likely been one of the very last interactions he would have with Aztlan in this lifetime. For a moment Tenuen wasn't sure he could breathe, let alone get up and commence whatever life was left to live.

All four knew very well that all life is eternal. One of the basic tenets of their education had been that leaving these physical bodies was not really an ending, but just a change in form. They had no doubt that death of one physical form was just the spirit evolving and moving on to the next experience, and that this had happened and would happen uncountable times to each soul. None of them had been shocked at the idea that Tia's spirit would one day live in a body of a woman called Sophie, thousands of years hence. And yet, even knowing what they did, the process of saying good-bye to this present life, to the people so dear to them now, was far from easy.

As they all cast about in their minds for soothing thoughts, Tenuen resolved not to ask a thing from his father during these final days. He saw that the king had little energy left and he, Tenuen, was ready to take up the mantle of responsibility along with his friends, sparing his father any additional strain. Whatever was coming, they would face it together.

When the attendant returned and asked the four if they required anything more, the spell was broken, and they began to stir and discuss the profound happenings in the upper chamber that earlier today none of them had known the existence of.

Persephone spoke first. "I think it was the walls of the traveling room that most impressed me. I've never seen anything like them. The depths of content in the twinkling light show!"

Tia found her voice as well. "Integra," she said excitedly, "the traveling chairs are so like our healing pod! The same synergistic effect of the crystals and the orichalcum. We must have unknowingly tapped into the same knowledge as the priests who fashioned those chairs so long ago!"

Then, becoming more serious, Tia went on. "So, the journey showed us a day in one of my future lives, when I will walk the labyrinth we are going to build. By doing so I'll be helping the generation alive at that time to turn back to the light. We must be sure it is built exactly according to the instructions we were given in Persephone's vision. It is clear how important the labyrinth is."

"I wonder who Ping might be?" said Integra.

"And where are the rest of us?" asked Persephone.

Tia, thinking and processing out loud, commented on how interesting it was that the Universe had shown them the future in the form of a stage play. Because isn't the entire world and all human experience just like that, anyway? People entering and exiting, the curtain rising and falling...

All at once exhaustion took over all four of the friends. More had happened in this one trip around the sun than any they could remember. It was time to rest. Tenuen stood, and noticing that he still held his father's scepter, he straightened to his full height and squared his shoulders. The three priestesses looked up at him and noticed how much he resembled a younger, more vibrant Aztlan. Quietly, yet firmly, Tenuen declared, "It is up to us now, friends. We have much to accomplish tomorrow. Let's regroup in the morning.

CHAPTER 18
AHNUHET

Tia had been sure she wouldn't sleep a wink after the day they had just had and with so much on her mind. Surprisingly, however, she fell into a deep and dreamless slumber immediately upon reaching her home. When she awoke, dawn was breaking, and as she stretched and opened her eyes, it all came swirling back into her mind. "At least I seem to have recouped some of my strength," she thought. "Who knows when I'll rest this well again?" She dressed quickly and made her way back to the pyramid building, keeping her mind clear of distressing thoughts as much as possible as she walked. She felt like a different, somehow older and wiser person than the happy and contented Priestess of Atlantis who had walked this same route on her way to meet Tenuen just a couple of days earlier.

Tia's arrival at Tenuen's chambers coincided exactly with that of Integra and Persephone, and they too reported having slept well and feeling ready to face the next challenges.

Tenuen's attendant met the three priestesses at the door and was laying out their breakfast just as Tenuen appeared, dressed in princely garments rather than his usual more casual garb. Tia intuited that her beloved was feeling the increased breadth of his responsibility very sharply today, after his father seemed to have stepped back and passed the mantle of taking care of the kingdom in its last days to his son. She realized that dressing in formal royal attire gave Tenuen a bit of a boost that was surely needed today.

The four friends enjoyed their repast before starting to discuss the business at hand. They ate fresh papaya and pineapple with coconut basted meats, and they drank the customary morning cacao tea, while engaging in only cursory conversation.

When the food and utensils had been cleared away, Tenuen started the meeting. He spoke slowly, with his head bent down. He began by remarking that they had loosely discussed dividing up the tasks at hand and accomplishing separate assignments. At that point, Tia broke in gently and suggested that it would be better if they acted together, as a group. "Our strength is in our connection and in our functioning as a team. Now, more than ever, I believe we must call on this strength." Tenuen visibly relaxed and lifted his head, his eyes sparkling his thanks to her for saying this. Persephone and Integra readily agreed, and feeling more at ease now, Tenuen continued.

"We will soon begin the process of informing the citizenry of the fate of our kingdom. Then we will begin helping each Atlantean with whatever is necessary for their journey to safe shores. I'm sorry for all the animals who dwell on the islands of Atlantis, but I see no alternative than to leave them to their fate." Seeing the pain in Tenuen's eyes, Tia moved closer to him and put her hand on his arm, offering what little comfort she could, feeling the same way he did about the non-human creatures of their kingdom.

Persephone said she remained hopeful about the potential survival of the animals. "The birds and sea creatures will likely find refuge," she noted. "I will do what I can to communicate energetically with some of them, but they will surely know, anyway, in their own ways, what is coming. They have more awareness than we tend to acknowledge."

Tenuen nodded and stood up. "Let's go directly to see Ahnuhet. We will bring him up to speed with all we have learned. It is time for him to know what is going to happen. I want to hear his wise counsel before we decide on the details of our next steps."

Ahnuhet, Commander of the Atlantis Navy, was the kind of man who always had things in hand. Though not a tall man, Ahnuhet was a distinguished and imposing figure and exuded a quiet dignity. His coffeecolored skin set off his sharp gray eyes, and his gaze was intense with focus and curiosity. When Ahnuhet decided to get a job done, it got done. "Ahnuhet knows what to do" was a common phrase on the lips of those who knew him. His actions and decisions were informed by his belief that being attached to any particular outcome only limited the options the Universe could provide. As head of the navy, Ahnuhet had interactions with a wide range of people and situations, some complicated and problematic, but he always tried to stay open and easy about things, and sure enough, solutions and plans would flow from his highly intellectual and creative mind. He never credited himself with the ideas, however. He always said the Universe was working through him, and that he was just the conduit.

When a messenger brought him word to expect a visit that morning from Tenuen, Ahnuhet was pleased, and not particularly surprised. As commander of the Atlantean navy he often interacted with the king's youngest son, who served as ambassador to many parts of the kingdom. Their meetings were always enjoyable and informative and the two had formed a relationship of friendship and respect over the years.

Leaving Tenuen's quarters, the four started on their way to the naval compound. As they walked, Tenuen mused that if anyone could bring order to all the chaos that was about to ensue, it was Ahnuhet. He voiced his feeling of comfort just knowing that he had a friend he trusted as deeply as he did Ahnuhet with whom to consult. The message he had sent ahead had been general and vague. It gave no inkling of the reason for their meeting or that there would be others accompanying him. It was only a short walk to the naval base, and when they were shown to his offices, Ahnuhet rose to greet them with a smile.

Atlantis had long been at peace. The kingdom had not seen military conflict for so long that most of the citizens had no memory of any. The naval personnel at the headquarters where Ahnuhet's office was located moved about with an air of relaxed readiness. Their training exercises continued to keep them skillful in the military arts, but with no expectation of needing to use them for defense of their kingdom. Ahnuhet, of course, being of approximately the same age as King Aztlan, did remember war. He had in fact long ago had to lead their navy into battle. But now, the overriding feeling around the naval headquarters was of lightness and ease, and he had no reason to expect that his meeting with Tenuen that day harbored anything out of the ordinary.

The sight of the three priestesses entering his quarters together would have raised an eyebrow had Ahnuhet been the type to show reactions on his face. But if he was in fact surprised at the presence of the women, Ahnuhet gave no such indication. Tia had previously met the commander several times, and Tenuen dispensed quickly with introducing Integra and Persephone, and Ahnuhet expressed pleasure at making their acquaintance.

The commander motioned for them all to be seated, and a sailor who functioned as Ahnuhet's attendant asked them if they would take a cup of cacao tea. Ahnuhet noticed that Tenuen seemed on edge as he waved the teapot away, stating that the group had just come from breakfast and was interested in getting on with the reason for their visit.

"Ahnuhet, I wish to begin this meeting by expressing my great appreciation for your expertise, your loyalty, and your dedication to the House of Aztlan and to the civilization of Atlantis. I and my three colleagues are here to give you information and to seek your guidance with regard to a matter of utmost importance and urgency."

Ahnuhet had never before heard Tenuen speak with such gravity and foreboding, and he inwardly braced himself for what he was about to hear. He felt a thought slip deftly into his consciousness, and realized in that moment that he had experienced a precognition or foreshadowing of this moment. He wondered in the next split second before Tenuen continued, if this had something to do with the forces of darkness, the recent turning toward false power-seeking and corruption on the part of some of the Atlantean people that he had barely been aware of and had not paid much attention to, knowing as he did that what he focused on would be sure to grow...

Tenuen laid out all of the details that they knew, including the fact that they had been instructed to build a labyrinth to save Atlantean knowledge and that they had been assigned the responsibility to save the citizens of the kingdom. As Tenuen spoke, Ahnuhet gave him his silent rapt attention, his posture and facial expression unchanging. Within, however, he registered the enormity of what he was being told, and his mind was working quickly as he thought about for what his own mission could be in all of this.

When Tenuen fell silent, Ahnuhet leaned back in his chair and exhaled slowly. Quietly but firmly he said, "With respect to the labyrinth, if you approve, I will take on that task myself. I will oversee its construction wherever my family and I relocate. I will bring top-level naval officers to help me. We will complete it as our final mission for Atlantis." Persephone smiled and said, "Oh, yes, this must be why in my vision I saw many military men building the labyrinth. In the vision my friends and I were not present at its construction. I believe it is ordained that Ahnuhet do just as he suggests!"

Ahnuhet then said, "The exodus from the Island of Atlantis is going to be an enormous undertaking." For the first time that

Tenuen could remember, there was, for a very brief moment, an emotional quality to the tone of Ahnuhet's voice. He recovered immediately though, and focused back on the practical. The commander had traveled during his lifetime to the outer reaches of the Atlantean world, but beyond the eastern edges of Atlantis was the vast unknown. If what Tenuen had told him was true, Ahnuhet reckoned that they must try to venture in that direction to save themselves and the other souls from destruction.

"We'll need more ships. With the capacity of our present naval fleet we would need to make at least three trips to evacuate the entire city of Atlantis. In the six moons time we have left we may be able to build at most three more ships, assuming no snags in the process, but even adding them to our fleet we would..." His next words were so quiet that only Tenuen, who leaned in closer, could barely hear, "...not save everyone." The color drained from Ahnuhet's face. He fell backward against his chair as if a strong gust had suddenly blown right at his chest, and he exhaled heavily. His eyes suddenly looking wild he looked at Tenuen and the three priestesses and then he breathed, "Please excuse me. I need a moment." Ahnuhet marched woodenly through a door in the back of his room and was gone.

The four friends waited for a few moments without speaking, and then Persephone, looking a little shocked, said, "It never occurred to me that we would not all be able to evacuate!" As if she had just now realized the enormity of the danger, she was close to tears and attempted to slow down her breathing and come back to equilibrium.

Tenuen became impatient when Ahnuhet didn't reappear right away and began pacing. After several minutes he excused himself and disappeared through the same doorway that Ahnuhet had used. He returned a short time later, and motioned to the women that they would all leave. "He has asked for some time, and I told him we would be back in the morning to reconvene our meeting."

CHAPTER 19
CRYSTALS FOR THE LABYRINTH

Integra had been thinking about the labyrinth ever since they received the directive from higher intelligence to construct it, and especially since the night before, when traveling out of body they saw the labyrinth as it would look thousands of years in the future. That vision felt like a validation of the way it had taken shape in her mind, and brought home with even more emphasis the vital importance of the mission. "My friends and I will directly affect the course that humans so far in the future will walk—we are going to gift them with the wonders and the brilliance of our beloved Atlantis," she thought. As they filed out of Ahnuhet's quarters, it seemed this could be the right moment to take her friends to the quartz mines to gather the crystals they needed, so she spoke up.

"Until we speak again tomorrow with Ahnuhet, let's suspend making plans for the evacuation. We could use the rest of today to put our focus on the labyrinth. The task of choosing the crystals will be more successful if we tap into the synergy of our collective intuition and energies. I suggest we go to the mines right now to choose the crystals."

Everyone agreed, and they set out walking through the

outskirts of the city toward the mines. As they left the buildings and paved stone walkways of the city behind, the rolling rocky hills looked deserted and wild. Integra knew exactly where to go, however, and she moved confidently in the direction of a particular large mound. They followed her along the dusty trail until she stopped at a place that looked at first glance no different than the rest of the terrain.

"Here we are," declared Integra, and she stood expectantly while the others looked around, wondering what they should be seeing. All at once two figures appeared, hoisting themselves up from what looked like a large hole in the ground. Integra greeted them warmly, and introduced them to her friends as brothers Anka and Zelft, the keepers of the quartz crystal mines of Atlantis. They were slight of build, had very pale hair and skin, and their eyes had a strange pinkish hue. Integra had always wondered if this coloring had resulted from generations of their family living underground and having almost no exposure to the sun.

When they weren't overseeing the mining of the quartz points and clusters, Anka and Zelft spent their time lovingly cleaning and faceting the crystals, and getting them ready for use in Atlantis. They lived in a cave dwelling built even deeper in the earth than the bottom-most mine shafts, and at the end of each workday they would go home through a natural tunnel, accessible only from the inner recesses of the mine. As far as Integra knew, nobody had ever visited Anka and Zelft's home, and she was always relieved when they didn't invite her to be the first. As much as she liked and respected Anka and Zelft, she did not relish the thought of an actual dwelling where the rays of the sun never reached.

Integra spoke directly to Zelft, as it was his job to curate and manage the Special Crystal Room. "Zelft," she said, "Please take me and my friends to the see the Specials." Zelft was very taken aback to hear this directive, since Integra had never before mentioned the existence of the Specials in anyone's presence but his own. The Special Crystal Room had always been a very well kept secret. Only Integra, and on rare occasions King Aztlan when he required a very special crystal, had ever entered it. Integra noticed the shock that registered on Zelft's face but she kept her gaze steadily on his eyes, and knowing it was not his place to question what Lady Integra instructed, he quickly recovered his composure, and nodded deferentially.

The group followed Zelft to a cave opening a short walk away from where they had been standing. Zelft stopped momentarily and took a small crystal globe from a bag he carried over his shoulder. He held it aloft to light their way as they continued through the opening and into a long, internal spiral walkway. At each bend, they descended two or three steps, and after several minutes of going around and down, Zelft stopped in front of a very large, black, arch-shaped door with enormous hinges. Set within that door was another door of normal size for humans to pass through. The smaller door was made of a light colored wood, and had no visible hinges. A green leaf that looked like a lily pad hung where a door handle might have been expected. Zelft placed his hand lightly on the leaf, and when he pulled it away they saw the leaf glow with a bright blue aura. Then Integra placed her hand on the leaf, and when she drew it away, the door slid open sideways, silently disappearing into the larger door.

Zelft beckoned them to cross the threshold into a room that was brightly illuminated by a dazzling display of large, clear quartz crystals. There were hundreds, perhaps thousands of them, lining the walls and floor of the room. The ceiling was at twice the height of a man, and each wall was several times that measure in length. It was the most wondrous site any of them had ever seen, and Integra smiled with satisfaction as she saw and felt that giving her friends access to this powerful room was having the desired effect. She had never even spoken to them about this place. Crystals were her passion and her profession, but there had never been a need to share many of the details about how they were obtained. Now, of course, everything was different. She and her friends all shared the mission to imbue crystals with energetic imprints so that they could preserve the precious knowledge of their civilization, and Integra knew that gathering here with all of them was the right thing at the just the right time.

Tia, Tenuen, and Persephone took it all in. Slowly, they walked around the room, gazing at the brilliantly faceted crystals that displayed themselves in every color of the spectrum and in every geometrical shape possible. From the tiny to the towering, each crystal was cut and shaped meticulously, the shapes themselves adding to the power, function, and capabilities of each stone. The crystals were formed when mineral liquid, deep in the earth, solidified into a crystalline matrix that perfectly repeated itself throughout. They presented as single six sided points as well as clusters of many six-sided points. These were then further faceted and carved by the skilled crystal workers guided by Zelft and Anka. The crystals were all quite breathtaking individually, but especially when experienced in such volume as was found in the Special Crystals Room.

The many different shapes the crystals were carved into fascinated Tia. She was familiar with those used often in Atlantean society for purposes of bringing light into dwellings, and she and Integra had ordered specifically shaped crystals for their healing pod, but the sheer vastness of the variety she saw in this room was beyond anything she had ever imagined. She gasped over and over again as each time she turned her attention was drawn to something more entrancing, more beautiful.

In addition to the crystals lining the walls of the rooms, there were many tables laid out with aisles between them. The crystals on the tables were arranged according to color, from sparkling clear, then purple, dark blue, lighter blue, green, orange, yellow, and finally fiery red. At the same time, if they put their attention on a particular crystal, they would see that it contained all of the colors together.

The shimmering and glowing crystals were energetically

broadcasting their agreement to be part of the overriding intention the group brought to the mines.

Tia stopped in front of a table piled with tube-shaped crystals. She was particularly drawn to one that was like a pipe that was longer than her arm with an opening twice as wide. She picked it up and felt a vibration come through her hand that felt alive. The crystal itself felt very light relative to its size. She looked questioningly at Integra who explained. "The carvers have been forming crystals into tube shapes that can be used as communication devices. It was hoped that a complete system would be in place soon for use by all of the kingdom's satellite settlements. The clarity of communication sent by this means is affected by the shape, size, and color of the crystal." Integra sighed. Not wanting to bring her vibration down with unhappy thoughts, she said, "We will take some of those on board our evacuation ships, so hopefully the project will continue."

After the friends had explored the Special Crystals for several minutes, Integra felt their collective vibration had reached the level necessary to complete their task, and she beckoned them to gather around.

"Persephone's vision did not include a precise plan for the design of the labyrinth, nor have we been assigned a specific number of stones to use. I believe though, that the crystals themselves will help us in our choice, as long as we remain open to their vibrational messages. The crystals will show themselves to be willing participants in the effort to preserve what is most vital about Atlantis. Let's walk separately and quietly among the stones and listen and feel the energy. I'm going to be keeping in mind that these crystals have a long distance to travel, and I think it's best that we each select only the size and number that we can carry unaided. Zelft will provide lengths of black silk cloth for wrapping our selections."

Tia, Tenuen, and Persephone nodded agreement, and they eagerly started to walk around the room again, this time listening and watching intently. The selection process went quickly, since just as Integra had intimated, the crystals that had grown in the earth for the purpose of being part of this mission let themselves be known by sparkling and vibrating and glowing in ways that were unmistakable.

A short time later they all brought their choices to a table that had been laid with silk, and were astonished when the accounting was done. Tia counted hers first. She had chosen forty-four crystals in all, in eleven colors, four different shades of each color. Integra had chosen thirty-three crystals— three colors, eleven of each color. Persephone had chosen twenty-two, and Tenuen, twelve. Adding them all up, the total number of crystals was 111. A sacred number, aligned and powerful. They looked at one another in astonishment. Clearly arriving at this number had not been random. They all felt strongly the hand of guidance from above, from their non-physical selves. They knew that while the labyrinth plan was not yet formed in their conscious minds, it was nonetheless playing itself out perfectly, as long as they remained open to this guidance.

They tied the crystals carefully into silken bundles, and slung their precious cargo onto their backs for the return walk to the city, where they had decided to put the crystals into Integra's lab in the pyramid building for safe-keeping. Integra wanted to thank Anka and Zelft, but they were not to be found, having retreated in deference and to give space and privacy to the prince and the priestesses as they went about the activities of their unusual visit. The walk back was quiet. Each of the friends was lost in thought. About that day's events, about the past, and about the future.

CHAPTER 20
AHNUHET AGAIN

Early the following morning, Ahnuhet's attendant was again escorting the group into the commander's quarters. This day, however, like the general atmosphere on the base, he was far less cheerful. Word of what had been shared with Ahnuhet the day before had spread quickly among the sailors.

As Ahnuhet opened the meeting, his stance seemed less erect, and his aura was less bright than usual. He did not invite his guests to sit, nor did he offer refreshment. Still standing, he began by apologizing profusely for having been so emotional the day before. Tenuen thought he had never seen his friend looking so diminished, and he quickly assured him that no apology was necessary and that they would pick up where they left off. At that, the commander's voice and posture returned to their usual assuredness, and they all felt his take-charge attitude had returned.

Directing his remarks toward Tenuen, Ahnuhet said, "I have already taken the liberty of beginning preparations for the evacuation of the populace, which I will implement at your agreement and direction." Tenuen nodded for him to continue. "I have spoken with my most trusted and talented men. As you know, our naval labs include one where we are learning about genetic material. Noakh, the head researcher there has made an interesting suggestion. We can outfit one of our ships expressly for the preservation of all the animal species alive on Atlantis today. By drawing sample genetic material from two individuals of each species—one male and one female—we can carry this material with us to our new land, and reconstitute the life forms there! I have assigned the manpower he needs to set this in motion, and we'll move forward with it if you agree." Ahnuhet's eyes shown with excitement as he delivered this news, and Tenuen, Tia, Persephone, and Integra were intrigued and hopeful at such an idea.

Turning to plans for the labyrinth, Ahnuhet continued. "As I said yesterday, if you agree, Prince Tenuen, I will personally direct the construction of the labyrinth. It would be a great honor for me to do so, according to the blueprint that you and your colleagues will provide me. I have already taken the liberty of choosing thirty of my officers who, together with the sailors in their command and their families, will sail with the crystals and everything we need for the labyrinth on board."

Tenuen let out a great sigh, realizing all at once what great pressure he'd been under, just beneath his conscious awareness. Now that Ahnuhet was fully on board he felt relieved and supported. "I do not doubt the brilliance of the team you have already pulled together, and I approve of all of the plans you have made. I and my colleagues are grateful to you and we know Atlantis is in the best hands possible."

At this, Ahnuhet smiled at the assembled friends, and asked them to sit down. Tea was served, and when the proper time arrived for the meeting to resume, Ahnuhet spoke again.

"Right away, we need to take an exact inventory of the vessels available, and how many each can transport. At your direction, friend Tenuen, I am prepared to send out my men to canvas the island and get the count we need, and at the same time to inform our citizens of what is tragically afoot."

"Yes, yes," agreed Tenuen. Please commence as soon as possible." Ahnuhet nodded to a nearby aide, who left quietly and swiftly. "And so, it begins," he said quietly. His heart ached as he pictured Ahnuhet's soldiers going from home to home, informing the Atlantean people of their fate. Standing abruptly, he began pacing with nervous energy as he exclaimed, "Ahnuhet, thank you for all that you have already managed to arrange. I appreciate your stability and your expertise. I know you have the tasks you have described in hand, and I await your report." The two men shook hands, Ahnuhet nodded to the women, and the four friends went back outside. Tenuen said he felt as good about everything as was possible. At least, he knew, they had the right man for the job.

CHAPTER 21
THE KING'S DECISION

As the four exited the naval compound to make their way back to the center of the city, they encountered one of Tenuen's attendants running toward them from the direction of the pyramid building. Out of breath, he stopped in front of Tenuen, and said, "Sir, your father, King Aztlan, requests that you come directly to his quarters." Tenuen thought it uncanny that at that very moment he had been pondering the fact that as one of the main stewards of the knowledge of Atlantis, Aztlan would take a big part in readying the crystals they had chosen for use in the labyrinth. He thanked the man and stated that of course he would come at once. The women decided to go to Tenuen's office to begin drawing the blueprint of the labyrinth, which they wanted to deliver to Ahnuhet, along with the crystals, as soon as the next day.

Arriving at the door to his father's chambers, Tenuen stopped and stared. He puzzled over the fact that the door to the upper chamber, which had suddenly appeared the other evening, was no longer there. The wall looked just as it had his entire life before their momentous excursion to the nonphysical realm where they had been shown a piece of the future. Tenuen's attendant nervously glanced between the place on the wall where Tenuen was staring, and Tenuen's confused face, and was about to inquire whether the prince required something before entering, when Tenuen pulled himself together, shook his head, and said, "Please let Father know I have arrived."

No sooner had he said this than the door swung open wide, and there was Aztlan, grinning at his son and reaching out his arms to take him into a strong embrace. Stepping back again, Tenuen took in his father's appearance and vibration. As he had at their last meeting, Aztlan seemed drawn and aged. His posture was still stooped. And yet, Tenuen felt that he seemed to have rallied a bit. The king now gave off a certain surety of a man alive with purpose. Some of the vitality that Tenuen had always associated with his father seemed to have returned.

Aztlan beamed at Tenuen and thanked him for arriving promptly. "Let's sit together here," he gestured to a cushion large enough for the two men to be comfortable, facing a low table set with fruit and cacao tea. When they were settled he turned to his son. "So," he said, "The crystals for the labyrinth have been selected and collected. That is very good." Tenuen made no response. He had long ago learned not to be surprised when his father had knowledge of things he could not have been told or otherwise reasonably learned.

Aztlan continued, "I have taken the liberty of fashioning some plans for the charging of the crystals with the knowledge of Atlantis. These plans involve the use of the traveling Room." Tenuen nodded, listening intently as the king continued to explain. "The center partition of the traveling Room that contains the chairs we used to travel out of body is fashioned from amalgams of particular metals and stones in specific ratios. Those seating pods were carved in such a way that when contact was made between them and human bodies, the formation of gamma frequencies is encouraged. This allows us to transcend our physicality. The floor of the traveling room is similarly imbued with the crystals and orichalcum, and a similar effect occurs when any form of natural substance comes in contact with these. So by placing the crystals on the floor of the traveling room, their energy matrices will vibrate such that they can more easily and fully be imbued with our intention, and with the information we want them to preserve."

Aztlan's eyes shone as he related this process, and Tenuen could feel the truth and power in what his father was saying, He just nodded his head in agreement, and was momentarily swept up in the feeling that they were all but small cogs in a very big wheel. He felt that events were unfolding under their own power, unaware and unconcerned with what he, or the other humans, were experiencing.

With no change whatsoever in his inflection or tone, and with no warning that he was about to make a momentous announcement, King Aztlan then stated simply, "And son, I have decided to stay in Atlantis. I will not take part in the evacuation."

At this, Tenuen's eyes flew open and he jumped to his feet. "But Father!" Aztlan held his hand up and went on in the same even tone. "I have thought long and hard, and I've made my decision. Like all of our ancestors, I know well the art of ending of a physical experience with peace and acceptance, and perhaps even with anticipation. I will welcome an effortless transition from this physical body, back into spirit form. This life has been long, successful and happy. I have neither desire nor energy to dedicate to the creation of a new homeland. I am leaving that to you and your generation. I choose to stay with my beloved land, and from here I shall go on without the burden of this well-used body. From the nonphysical realm, I will continue to love you and to guide you. We are eternally connected. In essence, as you well know, I am simply going into another room."

Tenuen sank back down into his chair. He was astounded and filled with emotion. His sadness was mixed with profound admiration for the man who had raised him, taught him, led him through life, and yet allowed him the freedom of expansion into his own destiny. For quite some time, Tenuen had perceived that the physical bonds that held his father in this lifetime were loosening, and that the earthly portion of their father-son relationship was shifting, ending. And yet, hearing the words, and witnessing the change in Aztlan's physicality, was astonishing, shocking even. Knowing that no verbal response was necessary, he did not offer one. Likewise, Aztlan did not try to soothe his son or attempt to soften the blow. He waited calmly, knowing that Tenuen would find his own balance.

Tenuen took a deep breath, and closed his eyes while he purposefully brought back the memory of a few short minutes earlier, when arriving for this meeting he had beamed the deep love and appreciation that welled up within him each time he was in his father's presence. By remembering the feeling he had the moment Aztlan appeared in the doorway to greet him, Tenuen was able to re-capture it. He took several slow, deep breaths, opened his eyes, and smiled. Aztlan saw that Tenuen had come back into alignment, and he too smiled. "I am proud of you, son."

With that he stood, signaling that the meeting was ending. Tenuen rose and as they walked toward the door Aztlan told him, "I have sent for Mira. She has responded that she will arrive before first light tomorrow. Let's gather here at that time."

Tenuen quietly let himself into his office quarters where the three priestesses' heads were bent together over a large drawing spread out on a table.

Persephone's friends felt they were lucky to have a teacher of her caliber in their midst, and they never minded that she sometimes sounded instructive or didactic, since what she taught was always fascinating and added to their lives in endless ways. Now, gesturing at the drawing with the piece of chalk she held in her hand, Persephone was explaining, "The labyrinth is an ancient symbol that denotes wholeness. It is designed as a circular path with spirals incorporated into it. There is no lack in the universe, and truly all is whole and perfect. But from our human perspective, lack might be perceived, and this gets us into trouble. The labyrinth will bring the gift of the knowledge of wholeness to the humans of the future. Those who walk its paths will have an experience of the unbroken eternal journey into the soul's center, out into the universe, and back again.

Tia looked up and noticed Tenuen standing unmoving near the door. He looked around the room, dazed and unfocused. Integra and Persephone followed Tia's confused glance and when all three women were looking at him, Tenuen said evenly and with flat emotion, "King Aztlan will be staying in Atlantis. He will not be evacuated."

With that, he walked across the room and took a seat at the head of the table and looked, unseeing, at the preliminary plans for the labyrinth that had been drawn. He sat woodenly, stiffly. None of them spoke. Each was absorbing the information that their beloved King would not be with them in their new life and land. Tia moved closer to Tenuen. Persephone rose silently and quietly called for Tenuen's staff to bring them some tensionrelieving tea. She wished she knew the formula for Mira's special tea, thinking they could certainly use it now.

Integra, ever ready to use the power and magic of crystals for any situation, removed a small red jasper stone from her pocket, thinking that it would help Tenuen to ground himself and rally. She closed her hand around the stone for a few seconds, and then reached for Tenuen's hand, which he absently opened in response, but the stone simply fell to the floor. Integra and Tia shared a look that said, "He is further gone than we thought."

"This news will take us some time to assimilate," said Tia, stroking Tenuen's arm. "We just need some time. We'll feel better as we go along with our plans." Nobody responded with agreement, and Tenuen didn't seem even to allow the words to penetrate his awareness.

Integra went to the corner of the room where a selection of

powdered incense and burners were always available. She prepared and lit a combination of lavender and other soothing essences, and when the aroma started to fill the room, Tenuen lifted his chest and attempted to breathe deeply. Slowly he regained his equilibrium. Tia could think of nothing to do to help him, and she was grappling herself with the shock of the community losing its leader, so she simply sat with him. The thought of Aztlan being gone from their experience was so devastating that she knew she had to keep it at bay for now, for Tenuen's sake.

Dinner was served, and half-hearted attempts to eat it were made, amidst mostly silence. When the scarcely tasted meal was cleared away, Tenuen seemed more his usual self as he began to speak. "Of course we have all been well versed in the way of life and death, and we know well that while the body is temporary, the soul is eternal. Indeed, we know that there is no death, really. And I know that I will rendezvous countless times again, in many lifetimes, with my dear father. But for today, we grieve. For today, we must assimilate the loss, for it is a loss that we experience now, in this lifetime."

Tia put her arm around him and squeezed gently. The group remained silent, which Tenuen appreciated. He knew they were all grappling with their own grief while at the same time respecting that his loss was the most profound.

Tia created a vision in her mind of well-being and peace, and focused there. It wasn't a completely steady vision, as distracting thoughts of what was happening in the here and now would come and go; yet like all of them, she felt her balance returning in fits and starts.

Tenuen cleared his throat. "Thank you, as always, my fine friends, for standing together with me. Tomorrow before sunrise we are to convene in my father's quarters. He has proposed that we use the traveling room to generate the high frequencies needed to imbue the crystals. He somehow knew that we have already chosen the stones for the labyrinth. Also, he has summoned Mira to help us. She is arriving before sunrise, so we will be taking advantage of the special energy of the dawn for our process of charging the stones."

Tenuen looked deflated and tired. He took his leave of the women, suggesting they all might retire early, as it would not be long before they were due to arrive back at Aztlan's.

CHAPTER 22
CHARGING THE CRYSTALS

The next morning, it was still dark when Tia arrived at the pier and looked out to sea, trying to catch a glimpse of an arriving vessel carrying her dear friend Mira. Everything about Tia's relationships with the people she cared about had taken on an urgency and intensity, and she hoped to be able to greet Mira and have her to herself for a bit before meeting the others at the pyramid. The moon was new, so the stars, having no competing light, glistened brightly. Not seeing any boats on the horizon, Tia looked up and located Sirius, her favorite star. Burning brighter than all the others, it was always visible in the night sky, and all her life, gazing at this star had given Tia a calm feeling of alignment. It reminded her of the eternal nature of all creation.

After waiting for a short time, she saw a small sailboat making its way toward shore over a calm sea. Tia knew right away that it wasn't Mira's boat, and she was momentarily disappointed. When it came closer, she recognized it as King Aztlan's private craft, one usually manned only by the king's designated top skipper or the king himself. When it was tied to the dock, she was surprised to see Mira bounce onto the dock in her usual dexterous manner. It never failed to amuse and impress, the way a woman of Mira's shape and size would veritably skip from a boat, having been, like most Atlanteans, accustomed to sea-faring vessels all her life. Today, in fact, Tia thought she detected even more of a nimbleness and quickness in her friend, and thought it curious that during what was truly a solemn time, Mira should appear almost lighthearted. She wondered too, why Mira had not come in her own boat. Why had Aztlan sent his personal captain to collect her? Those questions were immediately replaced, however, by pure gladness at seeing Mira walk toward her. The two embraced warmly and set off toward the pyramid building in the warm pre-dawn.

"I'm so glad you decided to meet me. Thank you," Mira smiled her affection for her young friend. Tia had her arm around Mira's back and squeezed her shoulder in response, pleased with herself for coming down to the docks in time to have this precious fleeting time. She had thought they might chat as they walked, but instead they fell into a companionable silence, simply basking in one another's presence. Tia smiled to herself at how perfect that felt.

When they arrived at the pyramid, they stopped for a hug before entering. Tia explained to Mira that the crystals she and her friends had chosen were in the laboratory, and Mira offered to help transport them to Aztlan's chambers. They entered the pyramid and hurried along the still dark corridors. Tia opened the laboratory door and was surprised to see that all of the crystals that the others had gathered were already gone. She and Mira hoisted the remaining crystals and when they left the lab, one of the king's attendants was waiting for them. Nodding his salutation, he turned and led them through back-hallways along the shortest route through the pyramid to Aztlan's quarters. Tenuen, Integra, and Persephone were already assembled in Aztlan's sitting room and were sipping tea, their crystals in their cloth coverings on the floor.

The king then emerged from his sleeping chamber, and Tia

saw Tenuen follow his father's movements with a concerned expression. Aztlan's posture was still a bit stooped, as it had been of late, and Tia thought she detected a fleeting look of surprise on Mira's face as well, although her voice and smile stayed steadfast.

The king greeted each of them individually, lingering just slightly in Mira's embrace. Tia and Mira were handed cups of tea, but before they managed to take their first sip, Aztlan began shepherding the group out again. They followed him back through the door to the corridor they had entered from, and Tenuen had to stop himself from exclaiming, "There's that door again - it wasn't here yesterday!" Instead, he just sighed. Nobody else seemed to have registered anything unusual, so he said to him, stifling a smile, "Well, this door to the upper chamber must simply appear on an as-needed basis." There was little time for all this pondering over the door, however, as the king seemed on an urgent mission. He wanted everyone up in the traveling room, and in position, before dawn had fully broken, to make full use of the power of the sun rising. Leading the way, again lighting the passage with the crystal at the top of his scepter, Aztlan moved as rapidly as he could and they all ascended, carrying the crystals, to the uppermost room of the pyramid.

Mira had given no indication of being surprised at any of what was transpiring. As far as Tia knew, nobody had shared with Mira their out of body travel experience. Tenuen noticed as well that the steep, dark passageway they were walking did not seem unfamiliar to Mira in the least, and when they arrived at the upper chamber and the king said, "open please", neither did she seem surprised at the traveling room itself, or its contents. Tia and Tenuen exchanged a questioning glance; each thinking it interesting that Mira seemed quite at home in this setting.

As night began to retreat and the first small slivers of sunlight sliced through the crystals in the outer walls, Integra cleared her throat and began to speak to the gathered friends. Her tone was somber, and she spoke quickly and quietly. "We are here this morning to infuse the matrices of these crystals with all of the knowing and experience that we have gained during the thousands of years that Atlantis has been in existence. The clarity of our focus and intention will be enhanced and magnified when we put those crystals into the traveling box. Each crystal will be encouraged to open its matrix and allow, easily and fully, the insertion and storage of the information."

Everyone moved toward the center of the room. Tia reached inside her robes and drew out four crystal wands. The wands were natural quartz points the length and girth of Tia's forearm; each wand had several long, thin orichalcum inclusions. Everyone entered the box that contained the traveling seats, and laid their crystals on the floor. As they did so, a pattern emerged. The crystals were laid in a geometrical design that optimized their energy transmission and reception. Tia noticed that it looked like a six-sided star, and was very beautiful to behold. She then placed the four wands at the four sides of the pattern, with their points facing out, and explained, "These crystal wands will serve as wave guides. When we instill information into the matrices of the crystals, the design of the labyrinth will be held within these crystal guides. This will help the builders of the labyrinth keep the design in proper mathematical alignment. We will instruct Ahnuhet and his people that should they become separated from the visual plan we will bring him later today, these crystal wands will have the ability to guide the building of the labyrinth."

When all the crystals were in place, Aztlan reclined into one of the chairs, and motioned for the others to follow suit. Mira fell naturally into place next to the king, and Tia, Tenuen, Persephone and Integra each took their seats, removing their shoes and placing their feet against the walls of the enclosure, as they had during their previous visit. Tia, who was next to Mira, saw her reach out to grasp the king's offered hand. Then Mira turned to Tia and held out her hand. Tia took it wordlessly, turned to Tenuen and locked eyes with him as she took his hand. He offered his other hand to

Persephone, and at the very moment that Persephone's proffered hand was taken into Integra's, the sun fully broke over the horizon and the room was illuminated with a soft glowing light. The 111 crystals on the floor sparkled and glimmered.

Suddenly Integra's voice rang out. She felt vocal sounds rise up unbidden from deep within her, and she intoned a long, continuous steady note. The sound was felt, as well as heard, by everyone in the room. Integra produced one tone after another, each one rising to a crescendo before morphing into the next. She felt as if the crystals were summoning energy and the sound frequencies she was emitting were facilitating the changing of the crystals' vibrations. As she chanted the tones, the others joined in, first very softly, then gradually more loudly with each tone. The six voices together sounded beautiful and powerful. After repeating this with several different frequencies of tones, they fell silent momentarily, and then Integra said:

"We call to us the powers of Earth, Air, Fire, Water, Plasma, and Ethers. We invoke the assistance of all these as well as any supporting powers, as we draw forth the entirety of the experience and knowing of the Atlantean civilization and instill it into the crystalline matrix of these crystal beings. We intend for these stones to recognize the optimum time to release this information at the request of humans of the future."

Tia felt the energetic fields of the crystals expand as they flashed with the most exquisite bright colors she had ever seen. She felt their presence as one feels the presence of other living beings, and her heart swelled as she received their communication of willingness and gladness to participate in the eventual continuation of Atlantis. Everyone watched the crystal light show in quiet awe, and with focused concentration they continued to beam their intent to the crystals. The orichalcum strips within the wave-guides were strikingly bright as they too flashed with color.

All at once, the crystals ceased their light dance. A constant, barely perceptible glow kept shining from within them. Tia wondered how long they had been sitting there. She felt disoriented, having lost track of time. Looking around, she saw that the sun was coming through the crystal windows on the southern wall, and realized the process had taken most of the morning. Suddenly she felt completely spent and exhausted.

Persephone and Integra stirred and sat upright. Aztlan was already standing, and he quietly walked to the door and left the traveling room. Mira finished putting on her shoes, and quickly followed him without a word or backward glance.

Unmoving, Tia watched them go. Looking around the perimeter of the room at the spectacle of lights that showed the vast sky on the walls, she thought this was likely the last time she would experience it. Then, not wanting to lose the high vibration of the crystal charging, she brought her thoughts back to how remarkable what they had just done with the crystals truly was. Yes, even for this group of Atlanteans, so highly trained in the ways of the non-physical Universe, it was a huge feat, and the satisfaction at having accomplished it was immense.

Tia willed her unusually heavy feeling body to rise, though she would have liked to lie still and rejuvenate a bit. As she slowly stood and stretched her arms over her head, her eyes fell on a small but bright light that was blinking on one of the walls of the traveling room, and she walked over to look more closely. When she approached, she realized the light that was pulsing its signal at her was Sirius, her favorite star. Looking at the entire wall of the traveling room, with its bright representation of the vast night sky, she felt an awareness of the enormity of the universe. Sending a wave of appreciation to the cosmos, she felt that appreciation return to her, magnified, carrying a profound message of peace and wholeness unlike anything she had felt before.

Turning, Tia noticed Persephone and Integra watching her, smiling. Tenuen came over to her and touched her shoulder, and he too gazed at the twinkling stars on the wall. The four friends began to move about, still in silence, as if sensing that speech would change the overall vibration in the room and bring the experience to an end. As they wrapped the crystals carefully into their silk coverings, their thoughts were reverent with the knowledge that they were preparing the stones for a journey to the place they would be found by humans far, far in the future, and would help those humans usher in a new era.

When the crystals were packed and ready, they carried them carefully out of the traveling room, and down the passageway to the main floor of the pyramid. After depositing all the crystals back in the laboratory for safekeeping until they could transport them to Ahnuhet, they all filed into Aztlan's sitting room. A spread of fruit and tea was waiting for them, and they all fell to eating with great appetite. Tia realized she had skipped breakfast to meet Mira at the dock, and it was now past noon. The silence was unbroken as they ate. When they were served the main course of coconut milk basted meats and fish, they emptied all the platters and bowls in short order.

When the meal was cleared away and a second tea service was offered, the four friends noticed that each person's tea, as it was poured from the teapot, was different. They recognized it immediately as Mira's tea, and they all wondered, but did not voice their questions, why this tea was being served here in Aztlan's offices. Tia saw that Aztlan himself was the only one, other than Mira, not seeming surprised by this. Tia exchanged curious glances with Tenuen and Integra, and Persephone kept pouring everyone more tea, enchanted with the yellow color that went into her own cup, and the other colors her friends were receiving. She especially enjoyed its special taste that until now she'd never had outside of Mira's home.

It was time for the silence to be broken, and Mira stood up and cleared her throat. Standing next to King Aztlan, she looked around at the gathered friends and said quietly but firmly, "I have something to tell you all."

Tia immediately had a feeling of dread, and wished she could stop Mira from continuing, but she knew she could not, and would not. Mira spoke in a matter-of-fact tone, as if informing them of something simple and mundane that was about to occur. "I shall not be joining the evacuation. This particular lifetime of mine has been long and happy, and I have fulfilled my purposes here. It is not my choice to participate in a dramatic watery exodus from this land, nor do I choose to be part of the creation of a new homeland. This is no reflection on my love for all of you. I will be with you always, whether physical or non-physical, and my love for you is eternal."

Tia, Persephone, and Integra simply listened to Mira's words. No response came to their tongues and their faces registered only sadness and shock. Tenuen had been watching Mira's face intently and when she finished speaking he lowered his head and nodded. He understood. He knew that like his father, Mira had made this decision from a place of complete alignment, and he would not attempt to dissuade either one of them.

Nobody made a direct response to Mira's announcement, and the silence continued. For the first time in her life, Tia felt uncomfortable sitting in Aztlan's rooms. She felt restless, as if it was time to move on, and she stood and motioned to Tenuen, cocking her head toward the door. He rose as well, and Persephone and Integra followed suit. Mira reached for both of Tia's hands and looked deep into her eyes. Wordlessly, the four friends parted from Aztlan and Mira with lingering embraces.

CHAPTER 23
THE EVACUATION PLAN

A moment later the four friends were standing in the hallway outside Aztlan's quarters. Everyone had risen early that morning, and the crystal ceremony in the traveling room had sapped much of their energy. Then, not having had much time to recoup, they had taken in Mira's news. Tia voiced what they all felt when she suggested they all needed a break. Tenuen nodded and started walking toward his quarters, and the rest followed.

Once inside the prince's office, the group sat down for a brief rest, but it didn't take long for them to regain their strength and for the momentum of their mission to return. Integra rose first and approached the table where they had left the drawing of the labyrinth. "We should get this to Ahnuhet as soon as possible." Her words seemed to snap Tia, Persephone, and Tenuen back into action, and everyone stood at once. They quickly agreed that the next step was to give Ahnuhet an opportunity to form an accurate picture of the labyrinth in his mind. The wave-guide crystals would be a big help should the original drawing be lost or damaged, but they all agreed it was vital that Ahnuhet carry the design of the labyrinth emblazoned in his consciousness as well.

Tenuen's attendant entered and was about to ask them if they required service, when all four friends moved quickly past him, headed to the laboratory to retrieve the knowledge-imbued crystals. There, they readied the crystals for transport to Ahnuhet, taking special care to secure the silken bundles. Tia, Persephone, and Integra tied some of the smaller packets to their garments, and the rest they hoisted over their shoulders. Tenuen carried the slate slab with the chalk drawing of the labyrinth in his arms.

On their arrival, they found Ahnuhet busy in his command module and the entire naval base buzzing with movement and purpose. When Ahnuhet looked up and saw them enter, his broad smile was quick and genuine and he came toward them eagerly. "You have arrived with perfect timing. I am pleased to see you all." His glance fell on the drawing in Tenuen's hands. "So this is the labyrinth I am charged with building, is it not?" He gestured to two of the men standing at attention at the perimeter of the room to take the slate from the prince and lay it on a nearby table.

Tenuen thought he noticed certain darkness behind his friend's smile and wondered if it was the enormity of all that was transpiring, or something else. Ahnuhet was in fact grappling with redirecting his thoughts away from those of the tragedy of the destruction of Atlantis and toward his knowing that all was unfolding as it should, even if it should not seem so to the humans directly involved. He knew that he needed to keep his head high and his thoughts focused. Having been entrusted with the building of the labyrinth and knowing its purpose gave him some hope and fortitude. He met Tenuen's eyes again and this time his smile seemed a bit more relaxed.

Ahnuhet ordered the room be cleared of all but himself, the prince, and the three priestesses. He proffered chairs around a table and he stood at its head. Ahnuhet looked at each of them in turn, cleared his throat, and declared that he was ready to give them an update on the status of plans for the evacuation of Atlantis.

"Although I have been charged only with the evacuation of the population of the main island, I have taken it upon myself to formulate a plan that includes efforts to guide and inform our satellite communities. I hope that will meet with your approval." Ahnuhet looked at Tenuen, who nodded for him to continue.

"I'll begin with a progress report on what has been accomplished thus far." Ahnuhet stood and clasped his hands behind his back. His face seemed to fall and age before their very eyes; his skin sagged, and his coloring paled. His voice became slightly lower, but he spoke clearly.

Ahnuhet told the friends that his sailors had completed their mission of informing the entire population of the main island of the coming disaster. In the process of informing the populace by going door to door, Ahnuhet's men had also gathered precise information about the availability of seafaring craft. Residents of the island who owned private boats would leave in those, carrying their families and as many neighbors as they could accommodate. Citizens who did not have private vessels would need to board the ships of the naval fleet. "We have also taken into account, Prince Tenuen, the capacity of the Royal Fleet, as well as your father's private craft."

At the mention of his father, Tenuen raised his eyes to Ahnuhet's, and he sighed. "I suppose now is as good a time as any to inform you, my friend. My Father will not be evacuating with us. He has chosen to stay on the island and to end his physical life when Atlantis ends its current cycle. The Royal Fleet will of course be at your disposal for the operation."

Ahnuhet raised an eyebrow in surprise, but nodded his understanding. There was a moment of silence while they all gathered their thoughts, and then Ahnuhet continued.

"As a whole, Atlantis has a population of approximately four million inhabitants. One million of these live here on the island, in the City of Atlantis, where we now sit." Tenuen and the three priestesses listened with rapt attention to their Naval Commander. "The other three million Atlanteans, as you know, are spread around the kingdom in various satellite settlements. Some of the settlements are just a day's sail away, while others require a sea journey of upwards of 30 days to reach."

All nine of Tenuen's older brothers were the rulers of satellite Atlantean communities. Tenuen thought about them, and especially the far regions of Carturrah and Azaroth, where he had recently visited.

"I seek your permission, Prince Tenuen, to send some of my men right away, on our fastest and lightest sailing vessels, to inform the citizenry of our satellite communities about what is to happen. The Atlantean communities that are built upon large land masses and on the coasts of continents will be able to evacuate their citizens not by sea, but rather by moving them inland, away from the tsunamis that will be caused by the comets hitting the ocean. The island communities will have to evacuate using whatever sea craft they have at their disposal. The advance ships I send now will rendezvous later with ours, as we make our way east."

Tenuen nodded slowly, again thinking about his brothers and their families and sending a silent prayer for their safety.

"Now," said Ahnuhet, "I come to the most difficult portion of my report." All four friends sat up straighter and leaned toward Ahnuhet to listen.

"I know we discussed this at our earlier meeting, and we all hoped it would ultimately, somehow, prove not to be true. However, we have undertaken a complete reckoning, and taking into account the sum total of all of the ships, fishing vessels, private pleasure boats, sea-going vessels of all kinds here on the main island of Atlantis, the situation is as I had suspected. We have the ability to evacuate only one third of the population of the city."

For several moments all four sat unmoving and silent, each perhaps hoping that Ahnuhet's declaration had been misspoken or misheard. Realizing they would make no immediate response, Ahnuhet pressed on. "Approximately six hundred thousand Atlanteans will have no means to escape the island. And the three hundred thousand or so that can be taken must somehow be chosen. My men have reported that some citizens, like your father, Prince Tenuen, have decided to stay. However their numbers barely make a dent in the total who will want to survive."

Ahnuhet sat down abruptly. Tia thought his expression looked surprised, as if hearing his own voice declare these facts made them real and undeniable, and he was feeling the full implication of them for the first time. But he very quickly brought himself back to professional dispassion and said, "I see no other solution but a lottery."

Tenuen, though struggling inwardly to maintain equilibrium, said evenly, "I agree. You are right. We have no choice. We will have to conduct a lottery to choose who will be evacuated."

Tia, Integra and Persephone sat speechless as they listened to the two men discuss the details of carrying out a lottery. They marveled at their ability to stay calm while talking about something as unfathomable as the end of Atlantis, where 600,000 people would be trapped and waiting to perish.

Tenuen asked the women if they would like a break before continuing the meeting. All three women wiped their eyes, accepted glasses of water from a man who suddenly appeared proffering them, and said they wished to continue. They wanted to hear the rest of Ahnuhet's plans for the evacuation.

Ahnuhet stood again, clasped his hands behind his back, and raised his head to full command position. "Now I would like to inform you of plans to specially outfit our largest and most secure warship. This is the ship to be used to transport genetic material of all Atlantean non-human creatures. The project is already underway, and the genetic material is being gathered as we speak. Noakh is in charge of this very important operation, and he assures me that the gathering of the material will be completed very soon. Noakh will captain that ship as well as oversee the laboratory on board where the genetic codes from all available species will be isolated, recorded, and preserved."

All four friends nodded acknowledgement of these plans, and Persephone and Tia both expressed hope that this would mean they would be reunited with the animal species of their island at some distant place and time.

Ahnuhet, hands now at his sides, walked to where Tenuen was sitting, and when Tenuen looked up at him, their eyes locked. The men had a brief but intense moment of facing their mortality and the reality of the perils of what they were about to embark upon. Then Ahnuhet walked back to the head of the table and both men returned to calm and professional demeanor.

Ahnuhet explained the general plan for the evacuation of the approximately three hundred thousand people they would be able to remove from the island. "We shall divide our available ships into two contingents, led by myself and Prince Tenuen. Each will sail with approximately one hundred and fifty thousand Atlanteans on board. I will captain our largest naval ship, heading east. We will continue on until we find safe harbor for the reestablishment of our community and the building of the labyrinth. And you, Tenuen, along with the priestesses, will take your father's largest ship and move in a northeasterly direction."

"Now, with regard to the labyrinth, from what we believe we know from the explorations of Atlanteans, it is likely that my group will find a land mass to settle upon soonest, and we will build the labyrinth right away. I see that you have brought many crystals for the project." Tia and Integra walked with Ahnuhet to the pile of black silk bags, and Tia explained that she had charged some of the crystals with the task of being wave-guides that would help him construct the labyrinth. They showed Ahnuhet each of the one hundred and eleven crystals, and he asked many questions, and when he was satisfied, they again put the crystals into their pouches. Ahnuhet understood that the labyrinth was to be built mostly from stone native to whatever land mass he landed upon, and that he could trust the process to unfold perfectly and in divine right timing, with the aid of the guide crystals and the plan that Persephone had drawn on the slate, and that Ahnuhet had committed to memory.

The group returned to their places around the table, but they all felt the meeting drawing to an end. There was much to prepare, and they felt ready to get on with the exodus. Tia looked around the table and said, "We don't know what our fate will be, nor exactly how the physical lives we are now living will play out." Tenuen's eyes again locked with his friend Ahnuhet's. "Perhaps it is destined that we should all meet after the coming event, and perhaps it is not. Let's not bid one another good-bye, for the souls of those of us who are true friends will be together again somewhere, sometime, in some form."

CHAPTER 24
AZTLAN AND MIRA

The four exited the naval area and began walking back toward the center of the city; Tia suddenly stopped and looked up at the sky, looking at a point off in the distance. Tenuen also stood still, and staring up at the heavens breathed, "did you see that?" Persephone and Integra followed their friends' gaze to a pair of bright pink lights, like fireworks, hovering above the tip of the pyramid building and they both gasped in disbelief and wonder. Tenuen cried a silent tear. Tia shivered as the lights became dim and disappeared, and then she bowed her head.

The four friends did not know, of course, what had transpired in Aztlan's quarters after they left that morning for their meeting with Ahnuhet. As soon as the door closed behind them, the king and Mira came into a long embrace. After several minutes Mira pulled away, and looking into Aztlan's eyes she said in a low voice, "Back to the traveling room, my love? "Aztlan answered, "Yes, one last time." And without so much as a glance behind, they made their way quickly up the passageway, hand in hand, to the upper chamber door. "Open please," said Aztlan. As they stepped into the room a bright pink light glimmered through the crystals. All of the celestial visions on the walls ceased their blinking.

King Aztlan and Queen Mira of Atlantis reclined side by side on the traveling chairs. Still holding hands, they conversed lovingly about their experiences during this time spent in physical bodies. Mira had always known that her life purpose was not to be in the public eye, but to work in the background to support the well being of Atlantis with her own special skills. Aztlan had always supported her life decisions, and they both marveled at how recently it had become abundantly obvious how advantageous was her choice to live as she had. When their talking ceased, their eyes met, and Aztlan said, "Thank you." Mira whispered back, "Thank you."

And then the immortal souls of King Aztlan and Queen Mira of Atlantis went speeding off into the universe, their laughter echoing throughout all space and time. Unfettered by the physical bodies they left behind, their spirits rose into the sky amidst pink arrows of light that could be seen above the pyramid of Atlantis.

CHAPTER 25
THE END

There was a palpable change in the energy of the great city of Atlantis after the departure of the souls of Aztlan and Mira. Everyone felt that an era had ended, and new beginnings were afoot for all, in different ways. Those whose names were drawn in the lottery were busy with packing and saying good-byes. Many had to bid farewell to family members, since the lottery was entirely random and did not take into account relationships.

Most of the citizens would not be part of the sea-going exodus, but rather, they would leave their bodies behind in Atlantis and move into the nonphysical realm. These people were preparing as well. Everyone was aware that during the coming autumn, now just a few weeks away, the comets were expected to hit, and Atlantis would be engulfed first in flames and then in water.

As they neared the time of departure, finishing touches were put to Noakh's laboratory and all of the ships' galleys were filled with supplies. Ahnuhet's men were finishing their inspections of the hundreds of ships and were ready to pronounce them fully prepared, when suddenly it began to rain. At first, nobody paid much mind to the rain, since Atlantis would often have daily showers in the summer, and they seldom lasted long. This rain, however, went on falling for hours, and then the hours turned to days, and still it there was no break in the clouds. After several days of this, there was a decided shift in the atmosphere, and what had been a gentle though constant shower turned into a heavy driving rain pelting down from low black clouds that made day seem almost like night.

The four friends gathered on the deck of the ship that Tenuen was to captain, and he announced, "We are ready to sail. As soon as the rain lets up, we will set forth on our final journey from Atlantis." Tia nodded, but just at that moment she felt an electric jolt hit her body. Tenuen saw her jump and moved to steady her as she swayed on the deck of the ship, which although still tethered to the dock, was rocking with the storm. Tia's eyes flew wide open and she seemed to be looking out to sea. Tenuen followed her gaze but saw nothing but driving rain and foamy rolling waves. Tia held onto Tenuen's arm and she had to shout over the sound of the rain as she told him, Persephone and Integra, "Mira appeared to me in that yellow

cloud above the horizon. She looked young and beautiful and she was smiling. I heard her clearly say that this rain will continue for forty days and forty nights. There will be no waiting for the weather to improve before we ship out. Let's go and tell Ahnuhet that the evacuation must begin immediately."

The next morning, still amidst a cold and heavy rain, under black skies, the four friends watched Ahnuhet's lead ship leave its moorings, followed closely by Noakh's ship. Then the rest of Ahnuhet's contingent of 300 vessels peeled away from their moorings one by one, and left the island of Atlantis, heading toward the open sea to the east.

Then it was time for Tenuen's group to leave. Because of the weather his visibility was limited, but he knew that his lead ship was followed by some three hundred other vessels of varying sizes, each piloted by one of the most skilled captains in Atlantis. They all left the harbor without incident, and they fervently hoped that as they sailed northward they would soon come into smoother waters.

For the next two days, as Tenuen's line of ships moved north, the rain continued unabated. Tenuen slept very little and stood at the helm almost all day and all night, his eyes on the sea and sky, in hopes of an improvement in conditions. On the third day at high noon, Tenuen was standing on the bridge of his ship thinking about how dark the sky was still, when suddenly an alarm rang out from the ship's crow's nest station. Tenuen looked around trying to discern the source of the problem that prompted the alarm, and what he saw caused his stomach to sink and the hairs on the back of his neck to stand up. He craned his neck forward in disbelief.

"That can't be possible!" Tenuen whispered to himself, and then he shouted an anguished, "NO!" In all of his many years of experience on the sea, he had only seen this kind of phenomenon once before. The sight before his eyes looked for all the world like what he had seen on his trip to his brother's province, when the man-made crystals had exploded in the water! He gazed in shock and disbelief at what was before him. "But we are far away from the lands of my brothers! How could the dark energies of those crystals of destruction have run amok this way?" Tenuen was breathless with desperation, but there was no time to warn the passengers or the other vessels, no time to turn back, no time for anything.

The sea churned—a violently swirling vortex of white foam on deep purple water. Giant walls of water shot into the air in a misty cacophony of chaos, grabbing the ships and setting them into an enormous hole in the center of the swirling vortex. The ships disappeared like mere matchsticks going down a drain.

And then they were gone.

Tenuen, Tia, Integra, Persephone, and the rest of the one hundred and fifty thousand people who evacuated Atlantis in their contingent. All were gone, swallowed by the sea.

Back on the island, the rains continued to fall. By the time the comets came and slammed down upon the beautiful capital city of Atlantis, the souls of the inhabitants who had been left behind were already in the non-physical realm. The Atlanteans, like Mira and Aztlan, knew that they could choose the time of their transition from physical to non-physical, and most chose to transition before the great disaster struck. They left only the empty shells of their bodies to be washed away with the coming flood.

The only citizens of Atlantis still in their physical bodies were those who had left in Ahnuhet's line of ships heading toward a new life to the east.

The comets' landed just as Mira had foreseen. They caused the earth to quake, and the walls of the city's structures to fall. The city lay in destruction and was engulfed in flames. Then comets fell into the sea, and the resulting tsunamis were so enormous, raising the level of the ocean to such height, that the greatest civilization ever known was completely obliterated.

Now, dear reader... That was the end of Atlantis, but not the end of the story. Souls are eternal, and in Book Two of the Time to Remember trilogy we'll meet Tia and her friends again, 130 centuries in the "future"...

ENJOY THIS STORY? If so inspired, the pleasure of a review is much appreciated! Thank you so much, and see you on down the road!

FREE GIFT

Thank you, friend, for bringing your focus this way! SO much fun to be in it together! Add more tools to your toolkit and continue your expansion as an intentional, masterful creator!

Sign up below and receive a new tool weekly for the next five weeks!

SIGN UP HERE:
https://bit.ly/deliberatecreatorstoolbox

SCAN ME

Made in the USA
Columbia, SC
30 July 2023